THE REMAINS OF THE WAY

David Boyle is a co-director of the New Weather Institute, and the author of a number of books about economics, business and the future, as well as history, including *Blondel's Song* and *Toward the Setting Sun*, about the discovery of America. He is responsible for launching time banks in the UK and has stood for Parliament.
www.david-boyle.co.uk

The Remains of the Way

The Pilgrim's Way mystery

David Boyle

THE REAL PRESS
www.therealpress.co.uk

Published in 2017 by the Real Press.
www.therealpress.co.uk © David Boyle

ISBN (print) 978-1912119721
ISBN (ePub) 978-1912119714

For my wonderful family, remembering ten years of walking along the Old Road, and without whom this book would not have been possible

I

"One ravine out of many radiating from a summit will lead to the one valley you seek; take another stream and you are condemned at last to traverse mountains to repair the error."
Hilaire Belloc, *The Old Road*, London, Constable & Co, 1904, page 5.

Adrian Matinson flicked his greying fringe out of his eyes as he wandered slowly, deliberately, towards his own front gate. He clutched his bag of fair trade coffee (Moroccan) and a copy of the *Daily Telegraph,* bought from the corner shop.

He always bought the *Telegraph* when he was on holiday. It gave him an almost erotic buzz of naughtiness. There was all that stuff about lawns and dinner parties and then, given the political complexion of his colleagues, it was hardly done for a Treasury civil servant to read it – and that gave him an enjoyable *frisson.*

He hesitated, and glanced at the distant view of

Croydon shopping centre, and then turned the key in the door. It was cool inside, out of the morning heat. With a sigh of contentment – there really is nothing like a week at home with nothing to do – he made for the cafetière.

There it was waiting by the sink – Adrian prided himself on washing everything up as soon as using it. He took the cafetière down from the shelf, put the kettle on the hob and turned the radio on. The referendum was in full swing: the 'Leave' campaign was holding its launch. "It is time to say no," said a familiar, grating voice. "No to the tides of foreigners pouring in through our open borders. No to the..." He switched the radio off again. That was more than enough for his week off.

At last, the kettle began to whistle.

As he reached across to switch off the stove, he glanced absently over towards the back door. Something was odd. The back door was slightly ajar. Had he opened it? He was almost sure he had locked it the night before. Perhaps one of his cousins had been in. As a middle-aged man, living alone, his cleaner came twice a week, but it was her week off too. He examined the door more closely, shut it tight and glanced around the room. Was it possible, he asked himself, that someone had slipped into the house?

There are luxurious games people play by scaring themselves when they actually know there is nothing wrong. That is what I'm doing, Adrian told himself. He walked nervously upstairs, and within a minute had glanced into all the rooms, behind all the doors and was telling himself off for over-reacting. Then he saw the open drawer in his bedside table.

He never opened it normally. But there was his passport lying on top, and his watch. Once more his heartbeat returned to normal and he walked slowly back downstairs. The television and computers were all in their places, yet something was not right.

He went back downstairs, sniffed the air and stopped still. There was a faint whiff of cigarette smoke. He never smoked and hardly ever had friends round and, when they did come round, they never smoked either. It was then that he saw the torn paper. He had walked straight past it in his hurry to reach the coffee. His post had arrived while he had been at the corner shop, and here it was – in pieces. Envelopes had been torn open. The contents had been strewn next to the doormat.

He bent down. All bills apparently. None of those envelopes looked as if they had contained cheques. He opened the front door again and looked down the street. The heat was rising and nobody was about.

But somebody had been here, within the last twenty minutes – someone who opened every one of his letters and then apparently disappeared, perhaps through the back door.

He turned quickly around to make sure nobody was behind him, reached into his pocket and pulled out his telephone.

It was only about quarter of an hour later that the doorbell rang. Adrian felt distracted as he tiptoed carefully between the torn envelopes, to reach the door. He had left them in case the police wanted to see them *in situ*. Could you get fingerprints from bits of old paper? He couldn't remember. He had already worked out that the contents of the envelopes were all there on the floor as well. Nor was anything missing from upstairs, as far as he could tell.

Through the glass of his front door he could make out a familiar blue uniform. He opened the latch.

"That was quick. I only called fifteen minutes ago."

"Phoned?" said the policeman, who looked unnervingly youthful. He hesitated on the doorstep.

Adrian realised he was drawing a long sigh of relief. He had been unable to convince himself that he was entirely safe. Someone had violated his sacred space, and torn open his mail. They might even still be watching from somewhere. He ushered the policeman in across the threshold.

"You look like you've had some kind of break in." He appraised Adrian uncertainly.

In the short period since Adrian had realised he was the victim of some sort of crime, he had veered from anger to fear – listening intently for a bump upstairs which would tell him he was not alone. The discovery that nothing had been taken increased his nerves. If the thief had found nothing then why had he left? Just because he heard the homeowner returning through the front door, that was enough reason for disappearing out the back.

As he steered the policeman into the kitchen, he looked nervously out into the back garden. Was that bush twitching? Was there somebody there even now?

"Mr Matinson, I've been asked to come round and see you by Hampshire Police. It's about your friend..."

Adrian turned swiftly away from the kettle and looked at him again. "You mean, you haven't come about the break-in? I thought you were joking. About the glass I mean."

Once again it was the policeman's turn to look confused. "I don't know about a break-in, sir. As I said, I've come at the request of Hampshire Police to let you know about your friend, Dr Peter Shilling. I'm afraid he's been found dead. In Winchester, in fact."

For the second time that morning, a great wave of electric horror coursed through Adrian's body and down to his toes. Horror mixed, perhaps, with a kind of inevitability. Of course, it would have to be like that.

The policeman's youthful face looked strained. He was not yet used to the business of breaking bad news and was uncertain what would happen next. "I believe Dr Shilling had no living relatives, and the local police asked me to..."

But Adrian heard none of this. The news that his friend had died was not entirely a surprise. He smoked heavily and was hardly in the first flush of youth, but he felt something had been wrenched from his own life as well. Pictures wafted through his mind from tutorials at university. At countless dinners and dinner parties. Long muddy walks. Postcards from obscure historic sites in dangerous corners of the world. Postcards, even in the last few days...

"Mr Matinson?"

"Yes, sorry." How could he have just gone like that? Was this the future for all elderly bachelors, and all antiquarian interests? To cease somewhere and have a policeman arrive at a friend's house, asking – asking what exactly?

"I'm so sorry to have had to bring bad news. Were you very close to him?"

"Well..." Was the policeman assuming they were in some kind of relationship? "Well, not in that way. I was very... fond of him." The policeman seemed to draw himself together.

"The reason I have been sent is to ask you, on behalf of Hampshire Police, to come and identify the body. There isn't anyone else. It is a formality, but a rather important one."

"How did you find me?" The policeman looked strangely nervous, and appeared to be consulting his memory.

"There was a diary in his pocket. It had his name in and your name and address as well."

Adrian could not concentrate. Why had the police, whom he had called about a minor burglary, happened to know about his old tutor? It all seemed too confused. As if in answer, the doorbell rang again. His feet scuffed across the torn paper and a gaggle of community police officers filed in. They seemed embarrassed to see a uniformed colleague already in the kitchen. They made themselves at home and he reached for the kettle a second time.

He began to understand. The young policeman

really had not come about the burglary. It was all a strange coincidence. "I'm so sorry, I've misunderstood the reason for your visit."

"Yes," said his original visitor. "Yes..." but he trailed off, staring into the garden.

Adrian remembered the next few minutes in painful detail, as if the whole fiasco had taken hours rather than less time than it takes a kettle to boil. He switched it on, using the moment for the news to sink in, slowly grasping and allowing himself to take some control of his emotions. He took a deep breath, turned round and began to explain to the police that someone had broken in through his front door, and there was broken glass to show how they had done it. He explained that the burglar had rifled through his post and then left, presumably by the back door.

He noticed, at this point, that all of them were staring into the garden.

"There seems to be someone still outside," said Constable Harris, the emissary from Hampshire Police. "You see that bush...?" The police filed outside again, dashed together down the garden over the unkempt, unmown lawn and lunged at the bush. Nothing came out. The kettle clicked off and Adrian, still nervously in the kitchen, reached for the mugs. Had he asked about milk and sugar? Too much had happened to keep everything in the forefront of his mind. It was then that he heard a muffled thud from upstairs. The police were the other side of the glass, preoccupied in the garden, but their presence gave him courage. He swung angrily out of the room and stood at the foot of the stairs. He shouted: "Is there anyone there?"

Silence.

Very carefully and almost soundlessly, he walked upstairs, one foot at a time. Half way up, a figure crossed the landing. He could see him quite clearly, a thickset man with a woollen hat pulled low and a paint-stained donkey jacket. The man stared back without apparent interest, as if Adrian was the one trespassing. It was a strange moment, haunting and fraught with uncategorisable fears.

"What the fuck are you doing here?" Adrian demanded.

For the third time, a cold spasm shot through his heart. For a moment, his conscious mind could not quite comprehend what he was seeing. The intruder's hat was pulled partly over his eyes and he was poorly, certainly inadequately, shaved. The man stared down at him, calmly and without malevolence, but with a disturbing confidence.

Adrian shouted out through the kitchen door. "He's here!" But he could see from the police down the garden that the shout had failed to penetrate the glass, and none of them looked up. A burst of adrenalin made him think faster, and he turned back to the intruder, wondering how to defend himself, but found it was too late. The man was already upon him. He had time to see the blur of movement in front of him and then the blow struck him full in the middle of the nose.

There was no immediate pain and Adrian felt himself falling backwards. The whole incident was happening so fast that he could barely put out a hand to save himself. The next thing he felt was a stunning thump on the back of the head as he fell heavily across the bottom of the stairs. The crash he could hear in the distance indicated that his attacker had already reached the front door and was gone.

Adrian slid down a couple of steps trying to breathe. All the wind had left him and he couldn't shout. He lay helpless for what seemed like ten minutes but was probably only a few seconds, trying to wrap his understanding around the events of the past hour or so, seeing himself objectively and without emotion. Then he put his arm down to push himself upwards.

One of the community policemen was there, and Adrian felt the urgency of the situation rush back at him. He gesticulated vigorously towards the front door. In a moment, the hallway was full of blue uniforms again, and people speaking on walkie-talkies or phones. There was a bleeping and a confusing chaos of limbs that were lifting him up, patting his head and asking him questions. Soon, the fatter of the community policemen returned.

"Must have took off," he said. "Did you get a good look?"

"Yes," said Adrian hopelessly.

"Might as well try a description," he said, without apparent conviction.

"Just give me a moment to get my breath back." Adrian breathed deeply a few times.

"Are you alright to come down to the station? We could call an ambulance?" He looked Adrian up and down as if checking his bodily status.

"No, definitely not. I really don't need an ambulance," said Adrian, and – feeling he needed to show he was not hurt – he got to his feet, felt dizzy and stumbled into the kitchen again. "I'm fine. Really. In any case, I have to go with your colleague to Winchester today."

"It's too late, sir, I'm afraid," said the thin community policeman. "I've already called one."

Throughout the painful process that followed, the shooting pain in his head as he got up, the ambulance arriving, fending off the ministrations of the nurses, Adrian could only think of one thing. Peter was dead.

He had known Peter for nearly three decades, since he was his history tutor at university. Their friendship began to play itself out, all mixed up together in his mind, as the A&E doctor poked at the bump on his head, asked him mathematical questions and peered into his eyes searching for concussion.

"How many fingers am I holding up? Mr Matinson? How many fingers?"

"Er, three."

"What is six plus three?"

"Nine. Really I'm not concussed. It was just a bit of a surprise, that's all…"

II

The scene was around Peter Shilling's gas fire in his university rooms, with piles of books and papers and candles in a combination that defied fire regulations, covering the floor around them. There is a warm smell of sherry. Then the dinners in Peter's dilapidated home in north Oxford. Then their walks along the towpath to various uncounted, uncountable public houses. Then their late night whiskies in recent years after Peter's wife had died and Adrian's relationship had finally unravelled in a welter of recrimination. And more and more.

He could hear his voice wafting down the years. "Here we are, Adrian, have a read of *As We Were*, by the brother of the man who wrote about Lucia and Miss Mapp, and see if it reminds you of me."

"Don't you believe it, young man. Economics is not just a handful of graphs. It is about making the words sing." It was true, as Adrian told himself, that his old friend was hardly getting any younger – a strange phrase, as if anyone short of Merlin had ever done that. He must have been approaching eighty, but still he had been able to carry out his very particular hobby, walking the Pilgrim's Way from Winchester to Canterbury and sometimes back the other way again.

All that walking. He was really pretty fit. He remembered Peter's staggering untidiness and his insistence on wearing plus-fours, almost a century after they had gone out of fashion. And his kindness, and so much else. No, he was used to vigorous exercise for a seventy-something, but he was not exactly fit – not after a lifetime of drinking and smoking to excess.

It was still hard to believe. All that learning, all that civilisation. Gone?

"Sorry?"

"I didn't say anything," said Adrian irritably. The doctor was taking notes. Constable Harris was sitting next to him.

"You said, 'it is hard to believe'," said Harris gently.

"I do apologise. I didn't realise I had said it out loud. It is kind of you to bring me here, but it really is time we both went."

"Well, take your time. We don't want to overdo it." The constable looked at his feet. He seemed immensely patient.

The doctor pushed his keyboard back. "Don't worry, Mr Matinson. Just a little while now."

"Excellent. Thank you. Let's go and do this statement and then off we go to Winchester." Things did seem finally to be moving somewhere.

"Are you sure you can't come back tomorrow? We can wait twenty-four hours before identifying the body."

Adrian got to his feet. It was time to finish this business. "I'll give my statement at the police station and then I'll come with you."

"Really?"

"No, I want to get it over with, if you don't mind. Nurse, I really need to go."

The nurse looked disapproving. "You are not quite yourself, Mr Matinson. You shouldn't be gallivanting around after a bump on the head like that."

By the time Adrian had managed to get the doctor to discharge him, and the official signature was firmly on his medical notes, and he had spent a wasted hour going through his description of the man on the stairs, it was mid-afternoon. He felt like he had been up for weeks and was resenting the loss of his day off. His head throbbed as they drove sedately through the traffic to the M3 and headed towards Winchester.

He found himself nodding off and woke suddenly. The engine wasn't running. He looked down through the trees and saw the squat medieval stone shape of Winchester Cathedral. PC Harris was sitting patiently next to him.

"Are you OK, sir?"

"Perfectly OK, thanks," said Adrian, struggling to understand where he was. The car park was strangely quiet. "Can you tell me something? How did you say Dr Shilling died?"

It had taken willpower to break the silence in the car now that the familiar hum and the comforting sound of the motor changing gear had ceased.

"I don't know, I'm afraid, sir. I haven't been told that information. They will let you know all you want to know down at the station."

They looked at each other for a moment. A lady in a blue dress and red jacket came past clutching her handbag. PC Harris started the car again and drove slowly back down the narrow medieval streets onto the one-way system.

Then it was the car park of the city hospital. The

policeman showed his ID card and they were ushered in through the basement to a green and white corridor, past a few patients in soft blankets looking white and abandoned on trolleys, in a haze of antiseptic and alcohol hand-cleanser.

PC Harris walked fast and Adrian still felt groggy. This was the second hospital he had been in that day, and he wasn't at all sure he shouldn't stay there. The truth was, his head was swimming a little. He tested out his giddiness, turning round quickly. Perhaps he did have a little concussion after all. For a moment as he followed Harris into a white room, he thought he was going to faint.

At least he was going to faint in the hospital. A pity it was in the morgue, he thought to himself, hardly able to take in what people were saying in rather quiet, understanding voices around him.

Before he had quite taken in his surroundings, the scrubbed workbenches along the walls and the thin swan-neck taps, an elderly man in a white coat had pulled the sheet off the mound in front of him and Adrian looked down.

Harris gave him an interrogative look.

"Is that enough?"

"Sorry?"

"Do you recognise him?"

Adrian looked down and focused. The truth was

that he hardly recognised this lump of inert clay in front of him, so white and unshaven. Peter's grey hair was unnaturally combed – he never remembered his friend's hair being this tidy. Nor did he remember him ever being quite so white, or quite so dead. Yet he did know for certain who it was.

"Yes, I do. It's him."

There had really been no chance it could have been anyone else, and yet Adrian felt a huge welling up of misery and disappointment. He could barely speak as Harris guided him humanely down the corridor and back out into the light. It hardly seemed right leaving the body of his friend in such bureaucratic limbo, but he couldn't think of anything else to do.

"Just a few formalities now, down at the station."

It was there, when he was finally signing his name for what must have been the tenth time that day, that Adrian asked the same question again. This time there were piles of dog-eared papers around him on the table.

"Tell me, do you know how he died?"

"I'm sorry, sir, I'm not at liberty to say that. I have no reason though to say it was anything unexpected at his age. There will be an autopsy and probably an inquest, so there will be an answer if you're patient. But he was what, eighty?"

"He was seventy-eight."

"Exactly. You've no idea how many of them conk out in the cathedral. There is something about it. I don't know." The jovial face of the desk sergeant seemed to imply this was some kind of joke.

"Where was he found?"

The burly policeman consulted the file.

"Well, I shouldn't say really, but just between you and me. He was found up in the choir stalls, on the right hand side. Just conked out, I wouldn't wonder. You don't know any reason do you? Any illness? Still, I expect we'll all find out at the inquest, eh?"

The look on Adrian's face clearly discouraged him and the sergeant drew himself up a little. "Knew him well did you? I gather he had no relatives living."

"I'm not aware of any illness," said Adrian. "Still..."

He didn't know what to say, but something was bothering him and he was unsure quite what it was. It was shocking that he had been in particularly close touch with Peter in the previous few days. Why had he not responded to all the phone messages which had arrived, in retrospect rather a peculiar number. Shilling had been doing what he so often did in the late spring, which was walking the Pilgrim's Way again, this time backwards from Canterbury to Winchester, and – in quick succession – Adrian had

19

received a number of calls and postcards. They were all a little cryptic, but you felt the wit behind them – and it was rather like Peter to play a kind of game with clues, especially as he was trying to encourage Adrian to join him. Or at least follow the same path himself. Adrian snapped himself out of the reverie.

"It's just that I had rather a strange postcard from him a day or so ago."

"Really?" said the policeman, uninterested. "Well, there will be an inquest, I'm afraid, which will probably call you. So we can go over all that then."

Harris dropped him at the cathedral, and Adrian thanked him. He felt they had gone through rather a lot together that day and felt a little empty without a policeman at his side. He promised Harris he would go home by train.

"Remember, go to the doctor if you feel any after-effects, sir," said Harris out of the driver's window. "In fact, go to Casualty, if I were you. Are you sure I can't provide you with transport?"

"Don't worry. It will be the rush hour soon. The train's fine."

"If you're sure then. Thank you so much. We're really grateful."

It had turned into a beautiful early summer's day.

There were elderly couples arm in arm, heading to tea shops, and boys ragging around in the dust outside the Great West Door of the cathedral, as perhaps they always had done. Underneath the huge, stone arches of the nave, cool after the sunshine outside, Adrian wondered why he had come. He knew there was no sense in this, but somehow the thought that his old friend had last been seen alive here preyed on his mind. It wasn't as if he really believed he would find traces of him; just that there was nowhere else to look.

He passed the stone memorials and *memento mori*. He paused to contemplate Jane Austen's grave in the north aisle, and sat in the choir stalls looking up to the great stained glass window above the high altar, and the ancient boxes above him carrying the bones of the Saxon kings, Alfred, Edgar, Aelfgifu, the human remains of a forgotten history. Here the sounds of plainsong had wafted over the coloured walls centuries ago.

Here the medieval pilgrims would have prayed before setting off on their pilgrimages. It had been on the right- hand side of the choir that Peter had died. That is where Adrian felt his steps taking him.

It was quiet and cool up there among the carved oak stalls. A battered old prayer book and a hymn book with four-part musical harmony were filed away in front of him. It was only now, in the relative privacy of the most ancient part of the old cathedral that Adrian breathed a long sigh and, out of his breast pocket, he pulled out a bundle of postcards, scratched and bent in the business of delivery. He had almost forgotten to bring them with him, the last thing he grabbed before leaving the house. He stared at them one by one, drinking them in as the last remains of his friend.

The writing was only too familiar, the fountain pen of antique design, the black ink, the exclamation marks and the familiar P to sign off, and on each of them a cryptic reference to a spot on his latest walk. Adrian had understood them immediately, or so he thought, as they had arrived one by one over the past week or so. He had understood that they had been designed to lure him onto the Pilgrim's Way, the Old Road the pilgrims took from Winchester to Canterbury.

They were the last contact he had with his old friend, and he longed for some kind of farewell, some kind of last acknowledgement, a final goodbye. Now Adrian looked at the postcards afresh, wondering if he could discern some final message. The trouble was, the remarks he found there, so typically tongue-in-cheek, made no sense away from the Old Road that Peter knew so well:

"Dear Adrian, Come on then! Pack your boots and get on the way, I'll meet you next week by the old cobbles and we can set off back the way I've just come. Yours till hell freezes, Peter."

Then there was the most recent card, which had arrived only a few days before. It was hard to decipher the rhyming couplet, which was presumably its purpose – to tempt him down. And he had sort of agreed to go, rather non-committally. He did have leave owing to him:

"You, thief, we know your name of course;
But who remembers now the name of the horse?"

It was a little impenetrable and, suddenly, Adrian was struck forcibly by the loss of his friend. Seeing his body had brought it home, but these hopeful, ingenious pleas for company brought back just how much he owed him.

For almost an hour, as the preparations around him continued for evensong, Adrian sat and thought back along his friendship – the kindness of Peter when he had withdrawn from the world, depressed about the loss of his wife of five years. The walks they had done together, along the Icknield Way and the Ridgeway. He had never quite done the Pilgrim's

Way. It had always seemed to be too close to summon up the effort, hardly even outside the M25 – heavens, it was inside the M25 for part of its route. You might as well walk along the Thames, or so he had protested. But it was all too clear from the tone of Peter's recent postcards, that one day soon he would put his reservations aside and walk the Old Road, after all. What a pity it would now have to be alone.

"Can I help you, sir?"

Adrian looked up. A very elderly beadle in a red coat was addressing him. "Only, we are about to start the evensong service. You are welcome to stay where you are but you looked so, um, distracted, that I just wanted to check you were alright."

Adrian rose giddily and thanked him.

"I'm fine. Thank you. Quite well. I had a bit of an accident this morning."

"Jolly good. So glad. We have had one person pass away here this week already. I didn't want to have another."

"You mean Professor Shilling?"

The man rocked. "I do apologise. Was his name in the papers? I didn't mean to gossip."

"No – I mean, I don't know. It was just..."

The beadle looked even more flustered. "Oh dear, don't tell me you knew him? I hope I wasn't speaking out of turn."

"Did *you* know him? Professor Shilling I mean"

The man's face softened. "Oh yes, I knew him quite well. He came here often. I used to recognise him and we often used to chat in the nave. He was usually in his walking boots. I was so sad he passed away, and I was here you know. I had just seen him."

Adrian's sprits leapt. Was this some kind of connection? "You saw him? How long before?"

"Well, it was a little strange. I saw him in the nave and nodded, but he didn't see me because he seemed to be arguing with a friend. The next thing I knew they were carrying him out of the choir stalls. I tried to find the friend, but there was no sign of him."

"A friend? I thought he was going alone?"

"Well, I assumed it was a friend. They were arguing about something. In fact, I heard Professor Shilling shout out in the nave. That's why I saw him in the first place."

"Really?" said Adrian. "What did he shout?" This was really very peculiar. He never remembered his old friend shouting about anything. Perhaps it was a case of mistaken identity.

"Oh, I remember that very well. He said: 'No you can't. Go away!' Or something along those lines. He seemed quite angry."

Adrian's head spun with questions.

"You told the police?"

"I did, as a matter of fact, but they weren't very interested. I'm sure it was just one of those things. Someone asking for money or something."

Adrian stared for a moment. That was probably right. The old man looked uncomfortable.

"I am so sorry to be the bearer of bad news. I hope you have a better day today. Are you walking yourself?"

"No, wait. Listen, Mr – er?"

"Fisher," said the old man shyly, looking around as if he had said something out of place.

"Listen, Mr Fisher. Can you remember anything about the man he was arguing with? Anything at all?"

The old man's brow creased. You could see the energy emitted from the effort of remembering.

"Oh dear, I am sorry."

There was a long pause as the old man stared pathetically into the middle distance. "He was tall, I remember that."

"Well, I'm very grateful to you," said Adrian, putting him out of his misery. "It's made a big difference to me talking to someone who was actually there."

"Well, I'm only sorry I could do so little. Wait!" Mr Fisher seemed to be struggling to articulate something. "Yes, I remember. He was very well spoken. Not the sort of thing you hear these days. Very posh. You know what I mean?"

Adrian's head still throbbed as he let himself into his own front door. The outer door had been boarded up. He must arrange to thank the community police who had been able to organise that. He felt utterly drained. There was still some broken glass under his feet, which scrunched as it bit into the stone flags. He looked down.

The post had been, as he knew to his cost. Yet here was another letter. Amazing how disorganised the post was these days.

He bent down and turned over the card, and he recognised the black spidery writing on the envelope. It was post-marked Winchester. Adrian shut the front door behind him and locked it, glancing down the street as he did so.

Then, on consideration, he climbed his staircase as silently as he could, and checked behind the doors and under the bed. Yes, then the shower curtain. Nobody there.

He took off his coat, looked nervously upstairs again before dismissing the possibility that the burglar might have returned, put on the kettle and sat down heavily at the kitchen table. He tore open the envelope. Inside was a postcard of Winchester Cathedral from the air. It seemed unexpectedly heavy. He turned it over. Sellotaped to the back was a small key, with a fob bearing the number 936, and above it in black ink were the words, written hurriedly:

"I think it would be safer if you hung onto this for a while. I'll explain when I see you."

He looked at the envelope again. It was postmarked the day of Peter's death. He must have posted this envelope before heading to the cathedral. Then it must have been delivered to one of his neighbours by mistake – it often happened these days – and they had put it through his letterbox later in the afternoon.

A peculiar thought struck him. Was it possible that the man with the woollen cap, who had seemed so worryingly interested in his post that morning, had been after this very letter? Did somebody else know that Peter Shilling had posted the key? He peered anxiously out of the back door. Then, taking the rolling pin out of the kitchen drawer – the first time it had ever been used – he tiptoed upstairs, put on all the lights, and looked again under every bed and in every cupboard. He went back downstairs and put the chain on the front door. Something strange was going on and he was too tired to work out what it was right now. But, in the morning, if he could drag his head through the night in one piece, there was some thinking to do.

III

"The unity of Europe, a thing hitherto highly conscious, fully existent, but inactive like the soul of a man in a reverie, sprang into expression and permeated outward things. Men travelled."
Hilaire Belloc, *The Old Road*, page 85.

The radio alarm woke him the next morning and Adrian tentatively touched his head. It still throbbed, but not as badly. Slowly, his consciousness began to concentrate on the cacophony of voices on the radio, broadcasting so close to his ear.

"We have been systematically fleeced by our European so-called partners and with the connivance of the ruling classes in this country, and this referendum is at long last a chance for the people of England to get their own back and send those foreigners packing."

Adrian dimly realised he was listening to the leader of the unofficial Leave campaign, who was clearly losing his temper.

"No, I will not – if you let me get a word in

edgeways." There was shouting and a couple of crashes in the background.

"I think Nigel is displaying all the imagination of the narrow-minded, bigoted little Englanders who have held this country back for so long. If we had listened to people like him for the past two centuries, we would still be travelling in stage coaches..."

It was one of the leading figures in the Remain campaign, Adrian couldn't tell which. There was baying in the background from the noisy audience. The BBC chairman cut in – it sounded like Jonathan Dimbleby – calling for calm. Then there was calm and a newsreader continued:

> "Those were the scenes before disturbances led to the end of the broadcast of Any Questions last night, the first time the programme has had to be abandoned in half a century of broadcasting. Police were called in to the ensuing disturbances and ten people have since been charged with public order offences. Two people were taken to hospital with minor injuries. Sir Nigel Jasper has claimed he was the victim of a deliberate plan by people he described as *agents provocateurs* and has demanded a public inquiry."

Ugh. Adrian flailed his hand around outside the

duvet and banged the radio off. It all made his head ache even more. He lay in the sudden quietness, breathing deeply and wondering what lay behind the overwhelming sense of dread he felt about the day. Then he remembered the white, clay body he had identified and the person who had gone from it. A wave of loneliness hit him and he threw back the duvet; he climbed out of bed, shaking his head and trying to return to the day. Jasper had irritated him, as he always did. It was time to go to work.

He took the postcards from Peter with him on the train and, as they trickled slowly through Clapham Junction, he took them out again and put them in order. The first four were conventional enough. It hadn't rained. Peter had forgotten his umbrella. He had a strange time in some Kentish pub. He had to dodge demonstrators from the Leave campaign in Strood. Then there was this cryptic message:

> *"I hope you're working hard, Adrian, so that you can join me on the return trip. I have left guidance behind me."*

He had been so close to seeing his old friend again, though he was far from sure he would have actually walked the Pilgrim's Way. He never had, and perhaps now he never would.

Then the card he had received before the terrible news. That was different somehow. It was written with the stub of a pencil. *"Adrian,"* it said:

"Things a bit strange here. Here is a clue for you now."

And then the clue he had read the previous day, and yes – still completely incoherent.

"You, thief, we know your name, of course;
But who remembers the name of the horse?"

What horse, for goodness sake? Adrian puzzled away at the clue as they struggled on past Battersea Park. It made no sense. He knew that his old tutor had loved puzzles and crosswords. He knew he foisted them onto his friends, and had promised to do so again when he lured Adrian onto the Pilgrim's Way with him the following week.

With a sinking heart Adrian realised, all over again, that was not now going to happen. For years, Peter had urged him to walk along the Old Road, and now – at long last, when he might really have been about to do it – it was too late.

But something was strange about all this. The key sent through the post. Was it really no coincidence that somebody had tried to steal his post yesterday? He shook his head at this latest insanity and tried to pull himself together. This was not the way a civil servant thought. He would leave it for forty-eight hours and then get in touch with the police. If there was anything strange in the autopsy, he would tell them about the letters. If not, well, he would leave well alone.

Just in case, he had crept out as soon as he was dressed and slipped the envelope with Peter's key inside under the lining of the small pond in his garden, before leaving home. It was the safest place he could think of.

All the way through St James's Park to his office in the Treasury, walking past the carefully weeded flowerbeds, he agonised about it. He worked those sentences this way and that, but from the moment he sat at his desk, turned on his government computer and fed in the complex series of passwords the system required, his attention wandered to more urgent matters.

The estimates for the new spending review had arrived, and some of them looked a bit bizarre. The report he was writing for the minister on the financial implications of the referendum was almost due. How would he have taken the time off anyway to walk the Old Road? It was almost a blessing in disguise that he wouldn't have to go.

For most of the week, he was back into the swing of things, thinking occasionally of Peter Shilling and who would arrange the funeral. He assumed his nephew would do it, realising suddenly that – if he had been the only friend – then the responsibility was probably his. He lifted the receiver and asked for the officer who had dealt with the case in Winchester. What was his name now? Harris, that's right.

"I'm afraid PC Harris has been transferred."

"Really, he never told me."

"I believe it was a sudden thing."

Strange. But there must be somebody else. There was obviously some confusion the other end. Finally, an authoritative voice came on the line.

"Mr Matinson? I've been asked to deal with any concerns you have. I'm very glad you rang. It saves us the trouble of contacting you. My name is Inspector Herd. You will be glad to hear that the autopsy of your friend showed nothing unusual. We must conclude that he died of natural causes. He was, I believe, nearly eighty?"

"He was seventy-eight."

"Quite. Now is there any way I can help you?" The

man's peremptory manner grated a little.

"I did have one or two concerns actually." Adrian jumped in before he could be prevented. "Mr Shilling sent me a number of postcards which seemed to show he was worried about something."

Now he had articulated his concern, he was sure he was doing the right thing. It only took a moment to put things into words...

"Indeed?" said Herd. He sounded thoroughly uninterested.

"I also talked to one of the beadles in the cathedral who said that, immediately before he died, he had been arguing loudly with a stranger."

"I understand that to have been the case. It may have over-excited him perhaps." That was certainly true. Adrian was nothing if not fair-minded. He weighed the evidence.

"I wondered," said Adrian, a little chastened. "Did you manage to trace the man?"

"No, we have decided to let the matter rest, in the light of the autopsy. We do have a number of demands on our time and, with all due respect, I think the evidence suggests that there really was nothing suspicious."

Adrian felt deflated. "OK," he said, breathing out. "Well, you are probably right." He felt relieved at this conclusion. "One other thing. Can you tell me who I should contact to arrange for the funeral?"

"The funeral? Well, you take me by surprise a little. I understand that took place yesterday."

If Adrian had been calmed by talking to obviously reassuring authority, this left him absolutely flabbergasted.

"Really? On whose authority?"
How could he have missed it?

"I'm so sorry, but there are occasions when we are asked to move quickly in these cases, and I was asked to speed up the proceedings. I am sorry that you were not informed. I can only think that was an oversight."

"Asked? On whose authority? Who asked you?"

There was a silence at the other end. There was the sound of a file being flicked through and papers sifted.

"I'm sorry, Mr Matinson. I'm not authorised to say. I can only say that everything was above board and we are extremely grateful for your co-operation."

"Yes, but..."

"Thank you so much, Mr Matinson and thank you again for your help."

Quiet but firm. Really ever so firm.

"It was extraordinary," Adrian was saying over coffee

in the Treasury canteen. "I'm not used to being quite so effectively silenced. I mean, I've done enough shutting up of people in meetings but this really overwhelmed me. I felt a bit of an idiot."

Adrian had taken to having elevenses with Nadia on Monday mornings and sharing the details of their lives. Nadia was technically senior to him, but they had risen through the ranks of the Treasury together. Nadia told him about the nocturnal habits of her children, their school reports and their run-ins with authority. His stories tended to be duller. It was years since he had so much as been out on a date, but he valued the connection and nurtured huge admiration for Nadia – especially perhaps for her golden hair.

"It sounds like you were cross," said Nadia. "I'm sure I would have been."

"You know it sounded almost as if he had been told to wind things up. But I can't help wondering about it? I mean who would want to wind it all up quickly. It's just an old man dropping dead in a cathedral. It must happen all the time. And you know how long it usually takes to get an inquest going."

Nadia nodded. She had run a Treasury review into the inquest system a couple of years before.

"It's very odd. You didn't meet him, did you?"

Almost none of Adrian's friends had met

Professor Shilling. His existence had become a standing joke to them. Adrian's mad historian. A dreamy silence fell between them as it can do for people who have known each other a long time. Adrian had been cross after he put down the receiver to the police inspector. He felt manipulated and he couldn't quite see why. But then again, he was trained to accept instructions and to carry them out, whatever he might personally think. Many of his ministers had been a good deal less polite than the police inspector. Perhaps that was just the way the public was treated these days. Heavens, he saw it everywhere – from doctors' surgeries to supermarket checkouts. Especially, perhaps, those giant call centres that seemed to dominate all their lives, run by the industrialist Jeffrey Steele, chairman and founder of the great outsourcing company, C4J.

Peter Shilling's rage at the doings of C4J felt suddenly brave and prescient. It made Adrian feel like weeping, thinking back to his friend's spectacular rants as they walked across ploughed fields or ancient churchyards, railing hopelessly at the modern world.

"Are you all right?" asked Nadia, looking concerned.

"Oh," said Adrian. "Yes. Of course." He pulled himself together into the Civil Service public face again – not exactly stiff upper lip, but knowing, amused indifference.

He pondered on the peculiar conversation with the police again as he trudged home from the station. The way these agencies treated people these days; it was extraordinary. There are probably 'systems' managing them, he thought. C4J's systems.

He reached into his pocket to fish out his front door key, pulled off his sodden boots and felt the familiar tingling sensation of doormat through stockinged feet. Then he looked down. There was another postcard.

Adrian dropped his coat and bent to look. He registered, as he did so, that it was another English rural scene. Could it be another message, from beyond the grave?

It was. With a sense of triumph, Adrian turned it over and there was the familiar handwriting, bigger than usual, rougher somehow, using what looked like the stub of a worn pencil. He thought he would never see another message, and yet here one was.

"Follow the way. Be careful!" he read.

Very peculiar. Adrian peered at the postmark. It

was difficult to read but it must have been sent a very short time before Peter's death. Why send him another postcard? What did this one add, except to reinforce the first message, with the added injunction to take care? Why did he bother? Perhaps Peter was just being forgetful; he *was* getting forgetful. But it was a useful addition to his collection, Adrian thought – special too; it sounded like a final injunction of some kind.

It was then that Adrian found himself imagining a journey along the Pilgrim's Way without Peter, a kind of final journey in his company, so to speak. It was the least he could do, a very personal send off. If his nephews and the police, between them, had conspired to keep him from the funeral, then he would conduct a funeral of his own – by doing what the dead man had asked him to.

As he imagined trudging along the open fields, with the North Downs to his left, retracing the old pilgrims' route step by muddy step, Adrian began to calculate when he would be able to go. There was the referendum report, of course. The committee would have to be postponed, but then he had planned to go originally with Peter. It must be possible to escape, if only for a week.

He fumbled for his mobile phone in his trouser pocket. Yes, there was Nadia's number. No better still, call Christopher, the departmental director. Yes, there was his mobile number too.

"Nadia? It's Adrian. Look, I am going on that walk after all, and I'm going to tell Christopher that you will be able to cover me at the estimates committee meeting. Is that OK? Could you possibly let me know? I know it's a pain but it would help me enormously. Nobody will expect you to know much. You can blame any omissions on me. I'd be ever so grateful."

"Go on Adrian, you deserve a break."

"Yes, I do, don't I? I do. Thanks so much."

Nadia was squared; now a message for Christopher explaining that he was, after all, taking the following week as annual leave and that Nadia would cover. He was free.

So it was with a liberated air of achievement and relief that he hurried to the pile of unsorted volumes in his front room. He found an ordnance survey map of the area around Winchester and tossed it onto the armchair. Then a guidebook to the North Downs Way. Where was it? A black volume, bound in plastic like a library book, as indeed it was – he had bought it from his impoverished local library for 30p a good decade ago. Clearly nobody had borrowed it for years. Yes, he could see it gathering dust again on his own bottom shelf.

He pulled it free of its fellows with a small murmur of gratification. Hilaire Belloc's *The Old Road*. He opened it near the beginning and read at random:

> "The sacredness which everywhere attaches to
> The Road has its sanction in all these uses, but
> especially in that antiquity from which the quality
> of things sacred is drawn: and with the mention of
> the word 'antiquity' I may explain another desire
> which led me to the study I have set down in this
> book: not only did I desire to follow a road most
> typical of all that roads have been for us in
> western Europe, but also to plunge right into the
> spirit of the oldest monument of the life men led
> on this island..."

That was more like it. Peter Shilling had sworn by Belloc. It was true that there was something about his prose, deliberately archaic, which seemed to touch something ageless about southern England, some historic truths too deep for articulation. For a moment it made deaths, even the prospect of his own, a small insignificant part of the greater life. In any case, walking with Belloc in his pocket would be like walking with Peter.

With satisfaction, and some relief from the sense

of gnawing grief and shock that had gripped him over the last few days, Adrian stepped upstairs to pack a rucksack.

IV

*"The Old Road was not paved; it was not embanked.
Wherever the plough has crossed it during the last
four hundred years, the mark of it is lost."*
Hilaire Belloc, *The Old Road*, page 75.

Adrian stood with his back to the Great West Door of
Winchester Cathedral again. The weather was
improving and there was a soft breeze on his face.
Above and around him, the gargoyles and carved
saints seemed to be holding their collective breaths,
as they waited for him to stride out on the memorial
path which ran diagonally over towards the high
street. In his hand, he held his battered copy of the
Old Road, with his thumb in the page which
explained that King Alfred's coffin had been sold for
£2 in 1788 when Hyde Abbey was finally
demolished.

He looked again and read out loud as if to an
assembled crowd:

"When noon was long past, we set out from Winchester without any pack or burden to explore the hundred and twenty miles before us, not knowing what we might find, and very eager."

Could he be described as 'very eager', Adrian wondered? His backpack was certainly something of a burden, but not too heavy yet. He looked up. People were staring at him, half interested, as if this was some forgotten ritual of the Church of England they had stumbled upon.

How many of these people would know about the Pilgrim's Way snaking off from here, going north-east or thereabouts all the way to Canterbury, he wondered? How many would even have heard of Thomas Becket and the four of Henry II's knights – Reginald FitzUrse, Hugh de Morville, William de Tracy and Richard le Breton – who murdered him on the steps to his own chancel in Canterbury? He was embarking down a barely visible, historic line across the home counties, but how many people could still see it – like a great spiritual spine, unrecognised, unvalued and largely ploughed over?

Get a grip, Adrian said to himself. He was getting like Peter Shilling. Why *should* they know? Nobody ever tells them.

He had woken early that morning and wondered,

rather late, what he should take with him. He found a small rucksack, put Belloc's book inside and another ordnance survey map he managed to find – a bit out of date: it still included branch lines which he knew must have disappeared in the 1960s with Dr Beeching. He found a water bottle, tracked down his asthma inhaler, added a notebook and his spongebag and shaver. What about teabags – well, why not? What about a jersey? It made sense. Soon there was far too much to carry. Wondering vaguely what else Peter Shilling might have included on a trip like this, he added in his small pile of postcards and headed for Clapham Junction.

It was these postcards that he felt inside his inner pocket as he strode forth from the West Door, and the sun burst through the clouds at that moment. People stood still to see where it came from and Peter quickened his pace up the diagonal stone path towards the high street.

He felt thoroughly alone. On his walking trips with Peter, somebody else had looked after everything. Peter's battered old rucksack, which seemed like a relic from the Boer War, had been copious enough to include anything they might have wanted – from bars of chocolate to whisky. This time, he was carrying too much and yet, every few moments, he thought of something he had forgotten.

His address book, no – something else... his razors...

There was also the question of an umbrella. The weather had been wet since the peculiar events in his house, and now the grey clouds had been gathering all the way down on the train and seemed likely to disgorge themselves on him as he strode along. Wading along the Pilgrim's Way – almost any Way in fact – would be enough to dampen the enthusiasm of any historian, let alone an amateur historian, and especially a holidaying civil servant.

"Going somewhere are you?" asked a man in a green jersey.

"Yes," said Adrian with a laugh. "I'm going to see an old friend." And straight as a die, he headed for the corner of the cathedral close where he knew he would find the shops.

He was aware as he walked that he had only a hazy idea of why he had come. He was thinking of his old friend every step of the way, and wondering if he was watching – hopefully with pleasure – as, finally, finally, Adrian had embarked on the pilgrims' path.

There was the paved area of the high street and the old cross, and here was the pavement, but he realised immediately that this was no ordinary shopping day. Two rival loudspeakers seemed to be vying with each other just up the hill. There were crowds carrying 'Vote Leave' banners, and further up the hill were the familiar yellow flags of the 'Remain' campaign. A line of police with helmets was emerging from the side streets.

As Adrian got nearer, he could hear what seemed like some kind of speech. It was hard take in the words.

"Britain has always been a European nation," bawled the activist into his loudspeaker. There was something familiar about the voice. "We've been part of Europe since the ice sheets withdrew. Long before the European Union. We have shed our blood in Europe and for Europe. Our opponents want to be little Britons, in some strange isolated island in the Atlantic. A bit like Atlantis, in splendid isolation. No trade, no culture, no friends, no nothing."

Yes, he did recognise the voice. It was... what was he called? Kenneth Baxter. Strange that he had been thinking of the old monster the previous day and there he was, bawling in some kind of loudspeaker car. There seemed to be an awful lot of union jacks. How extraordinary that people were so divided on the issue, Adrian mused, his civil servant's judgement coming to the fore. Hold on, what was this? There was a shout and from all around him emerged people with more union jacks and carrying red streamers, storming up the road.

A moment later, the first of them had reached the

loudspeaker and there were dramatic and muddled sounds of scuffling. "This is what happens when we hand the nation over to the nationalists," Baxter was shouting. "Tyranny... shall not... silence... mind control... thought... phhffhssss." The sound went dead and there was a great cheer.

Now the police were emerging in greater numbers, marching with shields up from the street behind him. On one side, the windows of Waterstones turned suddenly to smithereens. Somebody was throwing books. It really was high time he left, while he still could. Adrian ducked back into the cathedral close and, back in the tranquillity, breathed a deep sigh before heading eastwards.

Five minutes later, the sound had been completely blotted out by the buildings and he ventured back onto the road by King Alfred's statue, brandishing its Saxon steel. He saw with relief that he was now behind the police. He quickly crossed the road and roundabout, glancing up towards the inevitable and obvious melee in the high street, and headed round the inner ring road, past lines of gaily painted Victorian terraces, in search of Hyde Street and the first vestiges of the old way.

Somewhere around here, he knew thanks partly to Belloc, were the remains of what had once been Hyde Abbey, last resting place of King Alfred himself. The noise of the high street had died away but these obscure corners of Winchester were familiar, if only by repute.

He found he almost knew that the narrow road, called St Peter's Street, marked the spot where the church had stood, where they tolled the curfew in medieval times. He had been told so many times by his friend and teacher. Finally, there was the back street, called North Street, and there was the site of the abbey. He had never been there before, and yet it felt familiar, the abbey gate and the car parks and office car parks, which were stretched across what had once been the monastery grounds. It was in one of these spaces where Alfred's coffin had been dug up in the eighteenth century and sold for £2.

Adrian found himself wondering where the original road had gone. Where had those medieval pilgrims wandered exactly? Could he feel their distant presence, perhaps, if he stood in the right place? A silly idea. He dismissed it. But if the old North Gate had been at the top of the road, then the pilgrims would have carried on through Hyde Abbey or around the left hand side of it, down what was now Hyde Street. Adrian consulted his ancient guide. Belloc was vague on the subject, but all around him it was clear that this had once been a place of sacred activity – Nuns Street, Abbey Way. There was no sign of the pilgrims...

Even so, it was extraordinary to see what was clearly an old cobbled road and he wandered around the interconnected courtyards, modern business centres and 1970s housing estates and new brick-built homes with great wooden gates. There were bits of the abbey everywhere, but it was hardly clear what was what.

Where had they gone, laughing and telling their Canterbury Tales? In the excitement of the chase, Adrian momentarily forgot the purpose of the journey he had set himself – to carry out his friend's last wishes and follow the Pilgrim's Way, and perhaps pick up his friend's playful clues as he went. There, behind an obviously seventeenth century house, out of place alongside all those red-brick, Victorian railway cottages, was the locked gatehouse to Hyde Abbey.

Ah, the information board, said Adrian to himself – why do developers believe these are adequate replacements for what they have demolished? He walked round it, turned right into Nuns Road. There was no sign of the phone box which his other guide book had promised, but the way was obvious in front of him, going – judging by the sun – due north, in grassy muddy puddles alongside what was clearly one of the drainage channels that fed into the River

Itchen. It was all beautifully kept. The occasional tin marred the reed beds and the gently rippling water, and allotments ran down to the water's edge. The landscape rapidly deteriorated, first an abandoned smallholding with rusty corrugated iron. Then a dump for retired JCBs. Not quite the view that the pilgrims would have seen as they set out every July 31st *en route* for Becket's tomb, with the tales they were going to tell running through their heads.

The problem was the water. Even after a rainy May, it hung in murky puddles on the path, slopped over the top of the riverbank, sat in placid oceans stretching across the fields. But there was a calmness about the path, away from the disorder of the city, and – though there was no sign of the little bridges he was supposed to cross – the weeping willows along the way gave a sort of other-worldly dignity to the place. Adrian could imagine the pilgrims wending their way on the first day out, gazing as he was at the river, sizing each other up, excited but irritable in the heat. This was what Peter had seen each time; these were also his thoughts. It was a definite link.

But despite the wet, it had stopped raining pretty conclusively and Adrian felt his mood lifting for the first time since Peter's death. He could hear the sound of traffic from the Winchester bypass and glimpsed large lorries hurtling northwards.

When had he first heard about the Pilgrim's Way and his tutor's fascination with it? Actually, now he articulated the question to himself, he could remember precisely. There was a dinner party in Peter Shilling's flat, where he had lived with his wife until she decided to go and live in London. It had a bachelor air about it. There was dirt and dust all over the floor. The pictures had the dark stains of candle burns, from generations of student evenings gone before. There were piles of unreturned books from the college library in the kitchen where they sat around a white-painted table eating spaghetti and drinking red wine.

"Everyone must walk the Pilgrim's Way," he remembered Peter saying. "It is an absolutely compulsory element of being taught by me."

"Really," drawled one of his charges, old before his time.

"Why? Why? Because it gives you practice at deciding about the history behind everyday things, that's why. In the landscape, the trees and the way roads evolve…"

"Do roads evolve? Really?" somebody asked. Maybe it had been him. It was hard to remember across the years. Even at the time, those alcoholic evenings of his student days had dimmed the memory and slowed the responses, and furred the arteries too.

"Of course they evolve," said Peter getting very red in the face, as he leapt up towards the stove, which was smoking alarmingly. "The routes of roads survive when they are fit to survive. When they don't, people just go round and make the road somewhere else. If they get muddy or broken, then people bypass through the fields or the edge of the wood, and so the road evolves. The Rolling English Road. Who wrote that?"

Peter was never less than didactic, however alcoholic the dinner.

"Chesterton," said a girl next to him, who Adrian hadn't remembered really noticing before. "The rolling English drunkard built the rolling English road."

"Quite right," said Peter, eyeing her as if he wasn't sure who she was either.

She gave a little wink to Adrian. And now, nearly four decades later, that wink came back to him with all its original erotic power, and he stopped dead in the path, water flowing over the top of his bootlaces.

Of course. Barley. How could he have forgotten her, even for a moment? That was the night they met. Barley with the flirtatious air and endless successions of boyfriends, most of whom seemed to be called Rob. Barley, with the breasts which so obsessed him well into his early twenties. Barley, who became his best friend in his university days and afterwards.

Barley had known G. K. Chesterton's poem about the Rolling English Road because she had a mind like that, full of strange forgotten bits and pieces and peculiar bends and turns. Rather like he did himself. Barley, who read almost as much as he did, who agreed that neither could possibly manage to stomach Joseph Conrad. Or Deep Purple. Or Jim Callaghan. Or Margaret Thatcher, when she appeared on the scene during their university days like a Valkyrie.

Years of conversations with Barley in kitchens, on long walks, on hitchhiking expeditions, in motorway breakdowns, all flooded back as he took a deep breath of middle-aged regret and walked on. Blackbirds were circling the flooded fields, looking for drowning worms no doubt. He felt, for a moment, like a drowning worm himself. What have I done with my life? I never even slept with her – I barely even kissed her. And now look at me, doomed to follow Peter Shilling along the Pilgrim's Way like the Flying Dutchman.

He walked on towards the sound of traffic.

He opened Belloc's book again, and found the section on Belloc's own rules for finding the Old Road. They seemed voluminous but largely right. There were the telltale yew trees along the track. There were the religious sounding names of the villages along the way – King's Worthy, Abbot's Worthy, Martyr Worthy, Itchen Abbas, their meanings now almost forgotten, but presumably conveying something much more specific to the pilgrims.

But before he could reach the Worthys, something peculiar was happening to the path. Water now covered the fields as far as he could see. The guidebook talked about an embankment before the railway line and a wood, and a stile before the wood, where you could stand to see the line of the Old Road turning ahead of you to the west. Not only was there no sign of the railway, but it appeared to have been replaced by the bypass which was extremely busy.

When he reached the embankment and the roar of lorries, the stile had gone too, the wood had been replaced by offices – with company logos and slogans that allowed what the company did to remain entirely opaque.

Now he found himself in front of another underpass like a giant sewer. There were condoms under his feet and on the other side of the road. This was hardly an obscure way. It was clear that he had inadvertently bypassed the Old Road altogether, and he looked back at the unexplored outlines of King's Worthy to see what he had missed. A lorry hammered past and sprayed water over his left leg. He strode out along the tarmac towards Martyr Worthy and Alresford.

He had only walked for an hour or so, if that, and already he was exhausted. How was he going to make it to Canterbury? Still there was no need to walk it all at once. And in the meantime, he needed to sharpen his wits about the peculiar words that Peter Shilling had sent him.

"Who remembers the name of the horse?"

What horse? There had been no sign of horses at all since leaving Winchester along the drain that turned into the Itchen. Or had there been? Hold on, actually, there had been horses everywhere. The prime agricultural land had all but disappeared from this area and all that was left really was the detritus of pre-suburban living, a kind of horsiculture. Now he came to think of it, Adrian could see horses in all shapes and sizes in small paddocks, supporting small girls, lying on the grass, grazing gently in the fields.

He had now been walking for more than an hour and the transfer to tarmac was painful but faster. His boots whacked the black asphalt rhythmically, lulling him into a strange hypnotic reverie.

Yes, Barley. It was extraordinary that he hardly thought of her at all these days, when all those years ago at university he had thought about her constantly. He had worn one of her necklaces next to his skin as a private reminder of her – her long blonde hair, usually dirty and unkempt. Her complete failure to meet deadlines or assignations or dinners or to keep to any arrangements. The hours spent waiting for her and then forgiving her as she came laughing into view. The months spent enraged at the existence of some idiotic boyfriend. Called Rob, come to think of it. Why were they all called Rob?

Peter Shilling had often invited them both round to dinner, aware of Adrian's infatuation and wanting to bring the relationship to some kind of head. They could hardly have seen more of each other, but always there was Rob or Trevor or James in the background – Barley's latest inamorators, and he raged through the dinners. Why had he not simply demanded that he should be the one? She probably would have agreed to send Rob packing. Why hadn't he? Because at the age of twenty or twenty-one, he had not really possessed the words, let alone the confidence, to make such a declaration.

Adrian kicked the side of the road. It still fear it, after all this time?

He could see, to his right, the slope that Hilaire Belloc's book had led him to expect. The road might go up, it might go down and it might be flat, but it would always be on a slope, so that the water would run off – to avoid bogs. Down below in the Itchen Valley, he could see the medieval churches, always for some reason a quarter of a mile or so south of the road, for the pilgrims to turn off towards and rest. It was lightening into a better day, with patches of blue in the sky.

On the road itself were successive middle class mansions, some of them called Field House or Orchard Cottage, with expensive four wheel drive cars on the gravel, monuments to whatever natural feature had been there before the builders moved in, the linear descendants of the homes that would have lined the road as the pilgrims went by – and he could see why they might have wanted to rest, especially if the Old Road had been rutted and flooded, as it was now.

He began to long for a rest himself. There had

been many insignificant horses, but no sign of any significant horse. At Martyr Worthy, he decided to stop in the next pub wherever it was, but Martyr Worthy continued for what seemed like miles, detached mansions with their accompanying pine trees all the way along.

It was almost at the end of the next village, Itchen Abbas, that Adrian finally saw what he had been hoping for. The pub was called the Trout. He dutifully unpeeled his boots at the doorway and collapsed into a chair, pulled himself to his feet again and ordered a plate of sausages and chips. He stared exhausted out of the window. Nobody was around. Why had he not brought more reading material, for moments like this?

He felt light-headed and heavy-limbed drinking his fizzy water – he had given up alcohol for his fiftieth birthday, and not started again since – and waiting for his sausages. His arm brushed against the old bound volumes, clearly bought for their decorative value from some second-hand house clearance specialist. There were the complete works of George Eliot, a couple of books about tax law and a Victorian volume called *The Highways and Byways of Hampshire*. He pulled it down.

The great lumps of dust on the top made his nose wrinkle. Had he brought anti-histamine with him?

Almost certainly not. The book had clearly not been read for decades, possibly not even centuries. There was Itchen Abbas, in the index. The church had recently been rebuilt, said the book, but there had been a Norman church on the same spot and perhaps earlier.

Then he did a double take and read through the next sentence again:

> "The last man to be hanged for horse-stealing, one John Hughes, who went for his final drop in March 1825, is buried in the churchyard by the old yew tree."

Adrian stared and read it again. It was the first mention of a horse he had come across anywhere along the way so far. He reached into his jacket pocket and pulled out the wad of postcards. What was the clue again? Ah, here it was.

> *"You, thief, we know your name of course;*
> *But who remembers the name of the horse?"*

The sausages arrived and Adrian peered across the road at the church. He could just see its low, grey shape through the hedge. He re-read Peter Shilling's card, written with the stump of an old pencil. It might even be written with earth. It could have been, knowing the man who wrote it.

As soon as he had cleaned his plate, he pulled his coat back on and headed across the main road, through the lychgate and into the churchyard. There were two war graves, young men killed flying. The vast ancient yew was easy to see, much older than the church. In front of it was the worn and weather-beaten grave of John Hughes who died, it said, on 19 March 1825. Otherwise, the inscription was pretty much illegible.

But why had he been brought here? He peered more closely at the grave and the healthy-looking grass that covered it. Nothing. Then on an impulse he looked behind the gravestone. The earth had been slightly disturbed and something was glinting down there. It was the plastic lid to a small plastic tube. It looked like a medical sample bottle.

He dug it out and unscrewed the top. With a great feeling of triumph, he pulled out the rolled-up paper inside and laid it flat on his hand. The handwriting was unmistakeable. It was another clue.

It crossed his mind as he read it that his old tutor had gone to a great deal of trouble. Had he intended it as a game for him or was there a serious purpose behind it – or had it become more serious as the days went by? Did Peter have a sense that he was in some kind of danger, or had that come before the final note, in the cathedral itself? Had he been going ever so slightly round the twist? He read the note:

"I am old, Farmer William, the young man said: Follow him, Adrian, if I am dead."

V

"It was then our business to seek for some remaining evidences, apparent to the eye, whereby the track could be recovered."
Hilaire Belloc, *The Old Road*, page 103.

The thing was that Adrian had known immediately what the second clue meant. He knew it the moment he read the words. He was familiar enough with his old tutor's enthusiasms to know that. It was the second line that made him go cold with recognition.

Yes, it was true that Peter Shilling had fostered a morbid kind of fatalistic humour and was forever predicting his own demise. How many times had he said that he was about to trudge the Pilgrim's Way for the final time, or that his final bottle of port was about to disappear down his throat, or that he would dispose of himself with a razor if he couldn't find his missing copy of Frank Barlow? But, even so, that bald line – *"if I am dead"* – seemed to be so clearly intended as some kind of warning that it took his breath away.

A shiver inched down Adrian's backbone. He stood in the churchyard, the breeze blowing in his face, and stared out beyond the graves and across the fields, rooted to the spot. A frustrated choke of powerless rage overwhelmed him. Had my old friend been frightened? Should I be frightened now? No, don't be silly – I'm a government employee, for God's sake, a senior civil servant. I'm a member of the First Division Association. I'm paid a good salary, and an even better pension, because I'm able to sift evidence and not fall prey to the first conspiracy theory that comes along.

Peter's fear might perfectly well have been about his own health. Perhaps his heart had been playing up after the long walk. It had been unusually dodgy, even for him, and had been behaving strangely. Perhaps he had been getting his migraines again. Perhaps it was a tongue in cheek exaggeration. Either way, there was no need to get over-excited.

Still it was strange, that only – how many days was it after writing this? – two, maybe even one, that Peter was indeed dead.

Here's a possible scenario, Adrian rationalised to himself. Peter Shilling sets off walking the Pilgrim's Way for the umpteenth time, this time in reverse from Canterbury to Winchester, hoping to encourage his old pupil to come back with him the other way, and leaving these clues as he went to liven things up. Then, somewhere along the way, something happens – maybe he begins to worry about his health. Maybe something else, of course.

Adrian retrieved his bag from the pub and headed off along the route of the Old Road again. The clouds were looming ominously. Hilaire Belloc had been arrested in Alresford. At least he had managed to avoid that.

Could he reach Alton that night? He knew now where he was heading, and he could probably just phone for a taxi, but he felt somehow that his loyalty to Peter outweighed his laziness. What would Peter say if he was floating there above and could see him dialling the taxi number? And who knows, he could be – he always said that people survived death, at least for a while, and clung on to the earth, and Peter always struggled to keep his promises. No, it was time to press on before dark.

In New Alresford, he took a break. The light was beginning to fade. He had walked, what, ten miles? Maybe a little more. The road had become busier and busier and the lorries roaring past had begun to frighten him a little. On top of all that, there was the drizzle. He began to whistle the tunes systematically of Joseph and his Amazing Technicolour Dreamcoat, hoping that nobody he knew could hear him. Yes,

Peter Shilling had meant him to walk every inch of the Old Road to find the answer.

Was it Peter's idea of a joke, or was there some overwhelming reason why he should walk the road? Either way, he was going to find out. Despite everything, something was strange about these events in the last few days and he didn't like mysteries – he didn't believe in them. He owed it to his old friend to see the clues through to the end and follow the path laid down for him.

"Nadia?" He could hear her familiar laugh at the end of the line.

"I thought you were supposed to be walking to Rome or something. You should be out enjoying yourself." He could hear her giggle at the other end of the line.

"Ha ha," he said sarcastically. "It's so tough that I may soon be back. The trouble with the Treasury is that we don't get much experience walking through muddy fields."

"Through anywhere muddy, actually. We are a clean place, aren't we? Though I did have that chocolate pudding today. I haven't recovered yet."
Adrian had to laugh. They always joked about the Treasury's chocolate pudding. There were those who

said it could have been used to fill the hole in the nation's balance sheet.

Now, how was he to put this delicate request? It was going to take skill and tact, and might be best interpolated while Nadia was still in such a good mood.

"Listen Nadia, can you do me a favour? If it's at all uncomfortable you don't need to worry about it. I just thought you wouldn't mind me asking."

"Oh yes," said Nadia, with a world-weary voice. "Come along then. Ask away. I'm sure you were going to anyway, chocolate pudding or no chocolate pudding."

"You know the inquest people at the Home Office, don't you?"

Nadia was a little clipped. "Well, I did once."

"Look," he said. It was time to dive straight in. "Could you just ask them discreetly to look up about Peter Shilling's inquest and see if there is anything unusual about it? I'm still wondering why it was done so quickly. I'm sure it was fine and above board and everything, it's just that it's bothering me and upsetting my holiday."

"Oh heavens, Adrian. You do ask difficult things."

"It's just to stop me obsessing about it. You understand, don't you?"

"OK, but what reason can I say? Why might I be

interested? You know what they're like. They're a touchy bunch."

"Fear not, Nadia. I had a think about that. I wondered if you could say that you had received a request from the Cabinet Office because of a study they were doing on delays in the system – I mean, you could ask if it could be an exemplar. Could you find out what went right? You know what I mean. If they can speed up that one, why not the others…?"

"Mmmm. Not sure."

Really, honestly, why were civil servants so squeamish? "If you're at all uncomfortable… Like I say…"

"No, I'll do it Adrian, but you owe me, right. And not chocolate pudding either. I don't think I could take another one of them."

It was now raining and time to find a hotel. Outside the pub there was a white van, which looked familiar. There were two men inside in black anoraks. They appeared to be staring into space. One was talking on the mobile. For goodness sake, Adrian told himself, don't overreact. How many vans like this are there in Hampshire alone? How many in Alton? He noticed the small dent on the offside door. No, stop, stop.

This pilgrimage business could clearly send you

crazy. There was no reason, absolutely no reason, why anyone should be in the least interested in him. He had done nothing wrong. Peter had died, presumably of natural causes, an old man after some days of exertion. I'm a civil servant. I know things look peculiar sometimes but I also know most things in government, even local government, happen for an excellent reason. So stop being paranoid...

Could Peter Shilling have somehow arranged his own death in this way just to force me onto the Pilgrim's Way? Come on, Adrian, control yourself, don't lose touch with sanity, now...

He looked down the high street in the gloaming. Commuters were trudging home from the station. There appeared to be a steam engine on the sidings. It was time to find somewhere to sleep before he really started imagining things. There was a sign hanging in the breeze, marked bed and breakfast. The weather seemed to have turned windy and drizzly. There was really no decision to be made. He pushed open the iron gate and went in. It felt like a blessed relief, like a pilgrim on the Old Way welcoming his bed of straw.

Nearly a day later, every muscle in his underused thighs and calves aching, he came across the sign marked FARNHAM. He had walked all the way, past deserted pubs waiting for new owners who never came, and the lorries thundering by, and the signs to Jane Austen Country beckoning invitingly away from the task in hand. And as he struggled to still put one foot after the other, he thought over Peter Shilling's second clue again and again.

He knew of course what it meant. Farmer William could only refer to one saint in Peter's pantheon. If Shilling could have made one clue refer to William Cobbett, the great agrarian campaigner of the early nineteenth century, then he would have done so. Cobbett lived and died in Farnham. Farnham lay ahead on the Old Road and it hardly seemed a major surprise that there was a clue about him. Of course there would be. But there appeared to be some other invocation involved in the line: *"Follow him, Adrian, if I am dead"*.

Adrian considered the options. After all, he said to himself, it isn't quite clear what the word 'him' refers to. Am I called upon to follow Peter Shilling, and presumably not to paradise, but along the road? Or was I supposed to follow Cobbett – that made a lot of sense too? Didn't Shilling always enjoy paradoxes? Maybe he intended it to mean both – or perhaps he was just being lazy or he was in some kind of hurry. Following Cobbett would mean kicking up an almighty stink, because Cobbett, the great radical, could hardly open his mouth without offending the most powerful people in the land. Is it perhaps some kind of shaming comment on my job?

Peter never liked me kowtowing to ministers. He never liked the civil service mindset. Didn't he say that, if the Secretary of State wanted to gas people, we would write him an expert memorandum on how to do it more efficiently?

The prospect of following Shilling down the Old Road was simple enough. He was doing it anyway. It was in some ways the least Adrian could do. The prospect of following Cobbett to Parliament or beyond was much less comfortable for a civil servant. In fact, it gave him palpitations just thinking about it – maybe, like Cobbett, he would end up facing an action for sedition. I have to be careful. I have to navigate this with great care.

In any case, the real question isn't who I should follow, he said to himself. It is why Peter should have so accurately predicted his own death. Was it because he always expected to die after a little exertion or was it because he was genuinely scared? There was a rushed, desperate edge to the handwriting which seemed to imply something unexpected. Yes, something was going on. Everything in Adrian's background combined to make him look away, but equally everything else in his training – the balance of probabilities, the careful sifting of evidence – suggested peculiarities.

Either way, he knew where he was going. The William Cobbett. He would go there next morning and sniff around at this great junction of ancient roads.

Farnham was bustling with activity the next morning after he had washed and shaved and downed a cooked breakfast with extra sausages, which seemed to be *de rigueur* in B&Bs in this part of southeast England. There was a vigour about Farnham, which had seemed missing from the plush, respectable villages along the way. "At Farnham, therefore, the first political division of our road may be said to end," he read in Belloc's book. "And after Farnham the western tracks, now all in one, proceed to the Straits of Dover, or rather to Canterbury, which is the rallying point of the several Kentish ports."

It was when he was at the bar of the William Cobbett, looking across the inevitable horse brasses and asking for morning coffee – it was a little strange to find a pub like a coffee bar – that he felt the tap on his shoulder. He turned round. There was a lady about his own age with long grey hair and a big smile.

"Excuse me, but are you by any chance Adrian?"

Her eyes sparkled a little. He was Adrian, of course. There was no point in thinking too hard about it. Why am I getting so suspicious? Then a small suspicion in the corner of his mind began to grow. She did look familiar in the shape of her chin and her unusual nose.

"Hold on? Barley?

"Oh God, I haven't been called that for years. I'm Vanessa Modbury now, though I'm actually separated."

"Of course you are. Vanessa I mean. Was I the only one who called you Barley?"

She was as compelling as she ever was. A little plumper maybe, but it became her. A wave of nostalgia and frustration washed over him. How could he have let her slip through his fingers? How come he simply hadn't insisted that they get together? And now look at him, greying, careful, meticulous – the kind of man who wasn't really enough of a man for women to glance at him on the stairs of the Treasury. There was never a flash of interest from anyone in the glass lifts. Not a flicker, and he knew it and missed it, and all because Barley had flitted elsewhere, time after time.

"Well," said Adrian, feeling stupid, and unable to speak for all the sentences that had come suddenly into his head. "What are you doing here?"

"Actually, apart from having a cup of coffee, I'm looking for you." She smiled at him broadly and expectantly.

"For me?" It really was silly to feel that waft of pleasure.

"Well, you know it was a funny thing, but I met Peter Shilling here last week, or was it the week before? I ran into him, just like that. I've been living in Farnham for a few years now. I brought the children back from Spain when Rob moved out..."

"Rob moved out? I'm so sorry."

"Really?" said Barley, looking at him sideways. "Well, don't be. I'm not sure it was such a bad thing. It was pretty hard on the children of course. Still, his decision. Sort of..."

"You've got children?"

"Yes, three, they're nearly grown up – Jon, Adrian and Edith. Well, teenagers..."

"You didn't...?"

"Call him after you? I might have done, but mainly it was after his uncle – if you remember, I've got a brother called Adrian too." She laughed mysteriously and a little flirtatiously.

Adrian remembered suddenly what she had said. "You met Peter? Here? In Farnham? Do you know what happened?"

She smiled at him as if he was playing some kind of joke. "He was walking the Pilgrim's Way, I believe. Again."

She didn't know. He would have to break the news to her gently.

"Look Barley, sit down for a moment with me." He led her towards a bench and put his drink down on the table. "I'm so sorry but... well, Peter's died."

She stared at him. Tears came into her eyes and she blinked them away.

"I'm being so silly," she said. "I hadn't seen him for years, but somehow meeting him brought it all back."

"Really," said Adrian, aware that he was being ineffectual.

"How? I mean, how did he die?"

Adrian took a deep breath and looked at her. How honest should he be? There was a decision to be taken. He could lie and just say goodbye, but what would happen if he told her the truth – or told her his fears? She would probably get up and go and say goodbye anyway. Which way of saying goodbye was it to be?

"The thing is... It's a bit odd really. I don't want to sound hysterical or like some kind of conspiracy theorist or anything." He laughed suddenly. "Sorry, I'm being really obscure. The thing is I don't really know. He reached Winchester Cathedral and died there – you know he was walking the Way backwards? I had to identify his body. I must say, it has hit me quite hard. As you probably know, I'd seen a lot of him over the years."

"Yes," said Barley sadly. "You know, it's so lovely to see you, Adrian."

Adrian basked in the glory. She is really rather well preserved – far better than I am. She still has her astonishing figure. She still has a light in her eyes. What a waste. What a bloody waste.

"Adrian?"

"Sorry, yes?"

"I don't see why you thought it was a conspiracy theory. It all seems rather straightforward, doesn't it?"

"Well, it does," he said, convinced again that it did. "Tell me: what did you mean when you said you were waiting for me?"

"Because Peter told me you might be coming along. He said he was trying to tempt you, well, force you I think he said, to finally come along the Pilgrim's Way. I thought how lovely it would be to run into you and I've popped in here every morning since. Just on the off chance."

"Well, he succeeded rather well. Here I am. Well, he did, didn't he?" Right, it was now or never. "Tell me Barley... Vanessa, did he seem nervous or concerned or anything?"

To his mild surprise, Barley looked over her shoulder. "I tell you what. Let me buy you a cup of something."

The service was slow. There were rather a lot of mothers and toddlers in the pub that morning. The place appeared oblivious to them both, two middle-aged former friends, a little battered by life. A couple of old ladies next to them were discussing their late husbands' final symptoms. A couple of men by the bar were arguing about the referendum. Nobody was taking any notice of them, but Adrian saw her faint look of careful defensiveness. He knew exactly what it meant. Barley was confused about something. Maybe she had seen something after all.

They talked at the bar as they waited. Barley explained that she had been living abroad for a decade or so, that her three children were now taking exams and almost grown, and she had moved to Farnham to be near her parents, who had both now died. She felt a little stuck there. Doing some freelance marketing, selling cosmetics, trying to get into environmental consulting. She talked, and Adrian felt the years fall away. If I'm not careful, he said to himself, I'll find myself back where we started, back as the hopeless supplicant. She is still the same old Barley, a bit lived-in perhaps, but none the worse for that. I wanted to live in her myself, after all.

"Why did we call you Barley?" he asked. "Can you remember? It is three decades ago."

Barley laughed and pushed the greying hair out of her eyes. "Don't you remember? It was Peter. He was trying to persuade us to read Henry Williamson and Barley was his name for the perfect girl. Barley. Did you ever read it?"

Adrian shook his head.

"Nor me. But that was why. I rather liked it. It conjured up late summer and shadows and warmth and fields of grain. It conjured up the Pilgrim's Way in the 1940s, and the long hot summers.

"Yes, I liked it too. Though the Pilgrim's Way in the 1940s was a mass of defensive positions and concrete and wire. They were going to defend London from the top of the North Downs."

Armed now with coffee, they had reached the table in the corner. "The thing is," said Barley, abruptly changing the subject as they sat down, "I was rather worried about him. Peter, I mean. He said he'd been walking along the Old Road – do you remember how much he used to talk about it in the old days? And he said he was leaving clues for you, to lure you back in the other direction with him. That's right, isn't it? He said he was determined to get you to walk it once and for all. Then he said he had been a bit nervous because he had the sense that he was being followed."

"Really? Why did he think that?"

"He said there was a man in a white van who was always there."

Adrian felt impatient. "That just sounds ridiculous, doesn't it? There are white vans everywhere."

"The thing is, he said he knew who it was. He had been working on something or other about a very ancient and secretive government department, I can't really remember I'm afraid. Something to do with the Tudors. I wasn't really taking it in. You know what he was like."

The Tudors? This was getting ridiculous.

"The thing was that he obviously felt it very strongly. He kept on looking over his shoulder."

They looked at each other. It did sound important, but ancient and secretive government departments?

"I work for one of those," said Adrian. "It's called the Treasury."

They stared at each other, thinking hard. Adrian

caught himself glancing around the room.

"Look Barley, I don't want to burden you with this, but perhaps I'd better tell you the other end of the story."

It was only later, when Adrian had finished his conversation with Barley, and was walking rather light-headedly over to the bed and breakfast he had booked in a slip road off the high street, that he realised what had happened.

He had sipped his tea as he told her the story – the phone call, the trip in the police car to Hampshire, identifying the body, the peculiar way in which the inquest had been hurried through. He had explained about his strange day with the intruder just before. Then he told her about the clues, spread out his postcards on the beer-stained table before them and looked afresh at the story. He got out the strange note he had received at his flat, with its impenetrable message:

"I think it would be safer if you hung onto this for a while. I'll explain when I see you."

"What are you getting me into, Adrian?" she had asked him. He looked up and saw the amused, quizzical look in her eyes that was so familiar. They looked at each other; it was almost a moment of intimacy.

"Oh, don't worry about me," said Barley. "I'm in need of a little excitement at the moment."

She explained how trapped she felt in Farnham, her struggles to find work and the difficulties with the children – with settling in at their schools, with maths, with unreliable friends, the usual stuff so familiar with children at secondary school. Three decades were bound to take a little catching up. Their last meeting, maybe a quarter of a century before, had to be re-examined. Had he seen her off at the airport? Where had she been going? Where had she met Rob? Did they both remember that strange flat in Swiss Cottage? Who had lived there?

"What about you, Adrian? Are you married? Divorced? Separated? No? Surely not single?"

"I was married about fifteen years ago but it didn't work out. Kelly and I weren't really suited to each other. My fault. She got cross with me, and crosser as the years went by. In the end, she left. I still feel bad about it."

"Why should we both feel bad? It really isn't fair. I walked out, then he moved out, but, blimey, was there a good reason!"

"Of course I feel bad too. I suppose it takes two to

tango. I mean, to bugger up a relationship usually takes two people at least. Maybe more..."

"You mean, it takes two to break up a tango," said Barley definitively.

"Does it? I'm not sure."

The heightened sense of mild risk had made Adrian careless of what he said. Careful, he told himself. Just don't get carried away. But too much seemed to be happening and he suddenly felt he didn't want the conversation to end.

Looking back afterwards, as sat on his vast guest-house bed, with its cacophony of frilly pillows, he wished he had said more – wished he had reminisced about their evenings by the fire at Peter's flat and in his own room. How she had worn his undergraduate gown to skedaddle to the loo in the cold nights, with nothing on underneath. He wished he had asked, perhaps a little more boldly, about why she had never come back and never contacted him again.

But once again, Peter Shilling had come between them. It seemed frivolous to talk about anything else; his unused stove with the instructions still under the grill, his untidy habits, those dinners long ago and the succession of poseurs and dipsomaniacs who had joined them at those dinner parties.

"Many of whom I seem to remember you dated," Adrian had said, rather daringly.

"Nonsense," said Barley playfully slapping him on the arm. "One of them at the very most."

"Really, what about Rob the Knob?"

"He was the one, wasn't he?"

"What about Jeff from St Louis?"

Barley threw her head back and laughed. "OK, OK, stop, stop – enough already!"

It had been fun seeing each other again. They kept returning to Peter Shilling's dinners like an itch that needed to be scratched, and in between the sadness and suspicions about his death – sometimes concluding it was all a bizarre and unpleasant series of coincidences, sometimes something else – they began to find their way back into their old way of being together.

"But hold on a moment. What did you mean at the beginning that you were looking for me? Why were you looking for me? Because you wanted to see me?"

"Well, of course."

Then she leapt up. "Of course! I'd forgotten. I had a message for you."

Adrian stared stupidly. "Really? What?"

"Yes, yes, I had to point you in the direction for the clue. It's behind the bar, addressed to you."

Thirty seconds later, Adrian had been handed a grubby envelope. He tore it open. Inside was another of Peter's strange bits of paper. It appeared to have been torn out of a 1940s' exercise book. It had fading blue ruled lines and a red margin. The clue was scrawled on the other side:

"The northwest corner stones conceal,
Inside the lady of the wheel."

Wordlessly, he passed it across to Barley. "What on earth is that?" she asked. "That's not a message. It isn't even instructions. Is it?"

"Actually, I think it may be."

It was only later, as he collected up the clues and padded sadly off to his guest house, with a peck on the cheek to remember Barley by, that he suddenly realised.

Of course. The message that came in the post, and the key. It had come a day after the business with the intruder. Was it possible? Could they have actually been after the key?

He hardly looked at his surroundings, at the myriad of little cushions he was supposed to rest his head against, and the possibilities flooded through his head. He sat on the bed and stared out of the window a few feet away, various scenarios flashing up like film trailers. It was getting dark. Time perhaps to get a bite to eat. He must have been with

Barley in the William Cobbett pub until well into the afternoon, before she dashed off to cook something for her children. Achingly aware of the miles he had walked and his tired, painful thigh muscles, he pulled himself up towards the curtains. As he did so, he peered out of the window down onto the street. Then he stepped quickly back again.

Parked in the street just outside his guest house was a white van.

VI

"The alignment is continued through Puttenham Heath by an existing track, and in all this continuous chain there is no break, save the comparatively modern wall round the church."
Hilaire Belloc, *The Old Road*, page 161.

Adrian put his phone to his ear and listened to the familiar message. It was nearly lunchtime again, and a rare signal had appeared in the screen icon on his mobile phone. Why didn't Nadia pick up? He wanted to hear from her that everything was normal, so that he could set aside what seemed to him a very peculiar and debilitating suspicion.

Conspiracy theories were not his *metier*. He didn't believe in them. He prided himself on his hard-nosed belief that President Kennedy had been shot by a lone maverick. He knew Elvis was dead. It wasn't that there were no conspiracies; heaven knows, people conspired the whole time, it was that there were no *successful* conspiracies. Call it Sod's Law, call it the best laid plans, conspiracies were necessarily complicated and they didn't happen – life was too uncertain for that. He could hardly conspire himself out of bed in the morning without the world getting some kind of revenge.

It hurt him to find an exception to this rule, if indeed he had. He was enjoying the steady rhythm of walking and, the more he enjoyed it, the more this great exception – or the distant suspicion of an exception – preyed on his mind. It could not be so. Logically. How could an obscure and elderly retired lecturer possibly have attracted a full-blown example of something he firmly didn't believe in?

The problem was that, now this little doubt had begun to creep into his mind, conspiracies began to fill his waking thoughts. He had trudged in the pale sunshine through Seale and Puttenham to find the Pilgrim's Way taking an unusual sharp turn to the left, where the Old Road seemed to run slap into a high brick wall by the medieval church – the way past the southern entrance, which Hilaire Belloc said was the way the road passed every church, had clearly been blocked by someone or something.

It didn't take too long to work out why. Puttenham Priory, an eighteenth century Palladian pile, stands to the south. It is a giveaway, isn't it, Adrian said to himself. And Peter would have waxed lyrical about it and said that it was a giveaway in more ways than one. The priory was no longer there but must have been a medieval establishment to care for the pilgrims, given away or sold off to one of Henry VIII's cronies at the dissolution of the monasteries. The new establishment had simply enclosed the Old Road for their private use and delectation. And, judging by the clipped lawns, they still owned it.

Calm down, Adrian told himself, as he stared across the private grounds, and the Range Rovers in the drive. This is really too long ago to get cross about. Nearly five centuries. Even so, it seemed to him like a great original sin for the nation, a sin so great that the stain could not quite be washed away. He swung away to the north for the detour around what was now virtually a stately home, but had once been dedicated to God and the poor.

He was now in polite Surrey suburbia, in Puttenham Heath with its golf clubs and tennis courts and comfortable, red brick, Victorian villas, now rich with self-satisfaction and bankers' bonuses, and nestling in the foothills of the North Downs on the outskirts of Guildford. He trudged on down a sandy lane with the leaves squelching underfoot, pondering the clue which he had been given in Farnham.

"Inside the lady of the wheel." There was

something faintly irritating about these clues and their intensity, as if this had been a parlour game which had got seriously out of hand. Peter Shilling used to tell the story, which he insisted was true, of the four medieval friends who met for dinner and just for fun bet each other that they could walk to the Holy Land. Of the four, two died of disease, one became a pauper and one struggled home again. Pilgrimages were not for the faint-hearted.

There was a parallel here. A handful of clues, and here he was following them, giving up one of his valuable week's holiday when the man who wrote them was dead. Not only that, but he had managed to convince himself briefly that he was being followed. Despite his position. On the staff of the Treasury. A member of the First Division Association, for goodness sake. It really was ridiculous to feel so embattled about it.

"Inside the lady of the wheel." Was there some pioneer woman motorist whose name had escaped him? What about the Olympic cyclist? What was her name, Samantha? Victoria?

The evening before, he and Barley had met again briefly in the bar and had sat and puzzled together over the clue, still with the muddy finger prints of its author on it, and approached it from all different angles.

"If we could work it out, then you could cut a corner. Just get ahead to the end. Cut to the chase."

"I know this sounds silly, Barley, but I'm not sure I could do that in all conscience. I sort of feel like I'm doing the pilgrimage for him – maybe even *with* him in some sense. Do you see what I mean? I know it sounds a bit, what shall I say? Over-sensitive?"

Barley smiled. "Do you know what I've always liked about you Adrian? You take things seriously. Thousands don't. Millions don't, in fact."

"Really? I'm sure you described that same trait many years ago as 'boring'. I think that might even be an exact quote..."

"Nonsense. I've always liked it. I always did like it."

Adrian picked up the change of tense, but said nothing. He looked down at the clue again.

"You don't think it has something to do with lady cyclists do you? Wasn't there a line in Gilbert and Sullivan condemning the lady cyclist? I've got a little list. What was it? *The Mikado*?"

"No, it's some kind of sign, I reckon, the sign of the lady of the wheel. Perhaps it's a pub. It's either a pub or a mythological reference, knowing Peter. Or some combination of the two. No, Adrian. I always liked your seriousness. It was my fate to choose a man who wasn't serious at all. Still, it's over now."

"Is it? Where is he now?"

"Oh, he's around. In the City. On his yacht – he's taking the children to France on the yacht next week, in fact. Of course, I've got the children now, and I wouldn't have it any other way."

"Where are they now?" Was this a silly question?

"At school, of course. Or university. They're getting on."

It had been a silly question. Adrian kicked himself for his ignorance of such matters. Of course they were older than he realised. He noticed he was more pleased than he should have been that Barley liked his so-called seriousness. A warmth was spreading inside him which went beyond the coffee.

His steps were becoming rhythmical. Lunch was behind him and he had finally fallen into the rhythm of walking, his tired muscles compensating for the pain. I must not get excited about Barley, he said to himself. I must not get excited about Barley. Calm. Calm. Calm.

It was time to call Nadia again but there was no signal in this shrunken, overgrown, brambled path. Also it was almost time to cross the river. It was also time to stop and dig out his copy of Hilaire Belloc. He turned to the chapter called 'Alton to Shalford' and this is what he found:

> "Primitive man we must imagine chose, if he could, a ford, and kept to such a passage rather than to any form of ferry. The ford exists. It has given its name 'Shallow Ford' to the village which grew up near it. The church stands close by..."

Adrian walked down to where the ford had been and stared at the river. It was running fast and not very shallow at all. No wonder some would have preferred the ferry. In fact, the medieval ferryman must have been a tough customer. He remembered Peter Shilling talking about how notorious the ferrymen had been everywhere for their language and profanities. Hadn't there always been complaints made to the Archbishops of Canterbury for the way their own ferrymen opposite Lambeth Palace used to swear? The thought of it made Adrian smile again. As he watched the water pouring past, a bibulous evening with Peter and Barley wafted back to him over the years.

They had been talking about John Ruskin. A fellow student called Rob had been calling him the 'pseudo-sage' and Peter had been defending him as a great man and a great critic. Rob said he was a socialist. On the contrary, Peter had said, Ruskin had described himself as the most Tory of Tories – explaining that the one thing he claimed not to be was a Liberal. Barley had been there too, sitting next to Rob because, yes – Adrian remembered his irritation – Rob had his eyes on Barley and she had clearly melted, or was about to melt, into his arms. There had been too much red wine. He remembered taking Peter's side in the argument, though he knew nothing about it, purely to irritate Rob.

How amazingly cross these undergraduate arguments could get, when they were fuelled by wine and jealousy. For some reason, Rob had gone home earlier and Adrian had found himself around midnight, and rather tipsy, on Peter's front doorstep with Barley.

They had walked through the park and Adrian's inner voice had been shouting at him to act. But how? By the time they reached the darkest, shadowy part of the walk under the moon, the inner voice had become a scream.

"Barley," he said. She turned a bleary eye towards him and miraculously their lips seemed to move together. Adrian remembered it in slow motion. That strange feeling of the outer part of the flesh of her lips touching his, as he had dreamed of it doing rather too often. Her mouth opened.

I am kissing Barley, he had said to himself, unable to think of anything else. If ever he had been living in the moment, that had been it.

"It feels funny," she said. "You've got broad shoulders."

They hugged.

"Listen, Barley, it's my turn now. For goodness sake, leave Rob alone and be with me. It's my turn."

"Your turn? What a way to talk," she said, giggling a little. "I don't give turns. I don't line people up." She guffawed rather drunkenly.

"Yes, but he's a idiot. Pompous, pseudo-intellectual, pseudo-sage himself if ever there was one. In black shirts. Who does he think he is? Hitler?"

They kissed again. It was one of those dreamlike evenings, when you are young enough to feel that getting what you want is a magical business.

"I know you're right," said Barley. "But I'm going to go home now – alone."

"What? After all this?"

"It's just a kiss, Adrian. I know you're right, but..."

"OK, OK, promise me this. When you've finished with Rob, and God knows let's make it soon, then come out with me."

Three decades later by the banks of the River

Wey, Adrian scrutinised his younger self. What had she said? Could he remember exactly?

Had she told him to stuff himself? Or had she actually implied that she would do as he suggested – as he remembered? Or had she, actually, just said nothing and given him a meaningful look. He couldn't remember – but he did remember the wonderful walk home, in the firm conviction that they had some kind of arrangement. She had kissed him again on her own front door. Adrian remembered how erotic the taste of someone else's saliva could be, if it was the right person.

But, no, if there had been an arrangement, she certainly hadn't kept to it. He had not really been boyfriend material, he had to be honest with himself. He had long, greasy hair that he rarely washed and an awkward manner. Of course there had been no arrangement. How could there have been?

He sat in the Ship Inn to gather his thoughts, but they just would not gather. He tried to understand what Hilaire Belloc was writing about the mystery of where the Old Road crossed the river, but he could not concentrate. It was obvious that there was now only one way to cross for him, the footbridge at the end of Ferry Lane.

His mind still in another time and place, he sought the Wey. He passed the path up to St

Catherine's Chapel on his right and crossed the river, headed towards Chantry Wood and the growing cacophony of Guildford up ahead. The evening was drawing in and it was time to find somewhere to stay. He must have walked more than ten miles that day. He congratulated himself. His feet were holding out well, and he had met Barley, but he had made little or no progress with the lady cyclist.

His phone vibrated in his pocket.

"Adrian? It's Nadia."

At last. "Nadia, thanks so much for getting back to me. How did you get on?"

There was an ominous silence. "Adrian, I'm rather cross with you. You didn't tell me how sensitive this all is. I've had a number of difficult questions now and I think I've managed to wriggle out of it, but I may have got you into trouble."

Adrian laughed. "Well, it won't be the first time."

"No seriously, I don't know what is going on, Adrian, but I think you'd better stay well clear. I understand your interest in it all, but I had the Permanent Secretary at the Home Office phoning me up and asking what my interest was and I had to make up something about conducting an informal review. I had to claim ignorance and I said you were conducting it and I was just helping out. Sorry, Adrian, but he rather caught me by surprise."

The Permanent Secretary? That was very odd. "Strange. Did you find out anything at all?"

"Not much, I'm afraid. But I do know that the presiding government department at your friend's inquest wasn't the Home Office at all. It had the initials ODF."

His mind was blank. "ODF? It doesn't ring a bell."

"No, it didn't with me either."

Adrian ran quickly through in his head every government acronym he could think of. BIS, DfE, DH, all the great departments of state seemed to be known entirely by their initials these days. Nothing. It was disappointing. Why was Nadia such a stickler for protocol? But then I suppose we all are – that's why we are civil servants.

"Well, thanks Nadia. I'm extremely grateful to you. I'll just have to poke round and find out what ODF stands for."

"I've done that."

His heart leapt. "You have?"

"Yes, it wasn't listed in any of the government directories or on the gov.uk website. I've only been able to discover this because the Treasury makes an annual subvention to them of £10.4 million a year and that's listed simply as 'Sundries, ODF'."

"Strange..." echoed Adrian

"And even then it is in a list of transfers that I

shouldn't have accessed."

"Really, Nadia, I owe you big time for this."
"I looked for the file online and it wasn't there, so I asked Karen."

Ah, Karen. What a good idea. Karen was an elderly functionary who doled out stores and appeared to know everything.

" 'ODF,' she said to herself. You know how she talks. 'ODF? I don't know, dear, it rings a bell'..."

Adrian laughed politely at Nadia's imitation.

"And?" Good lord, Nadia did beat around the bush. He was having difficulty hearing her now he had crossed the railway junction, walked through the roundabout and up into the high street. Why did people look so drab in Guildford? It was all very strange.

"Anyway, she remembered ODF."

"And, what did she say? What does it stand for?"

"She didn't know. She only knew that because, years ago, there had been some difficulty about the subvention not getting through. But it did spell out what the money was for."

Adrian pricked up his ears.

"That's the odd part," she was saying. "It was for fireworks, rockets, sparklers, Catherine wheels and so on, and other support for Guy Fawkes Day, at least that's how it was recorded."

"Why was a government department buying fireworks?"

"Maybe there was some link to the parks or the Royal Palaces, I don't know, really. Could be any number of things."

"How bizarre, Nadia. What do *you* think?"

"Me? You want to know what I think? Well, Adrian, I think you should leave well alone. Really. It won't help your career if you go nosing around in someone else's business."

Adrian knew immediately that she was right. So why was he continuing to nose around, he asked himself? Why take these risks with his career as a civil servant."

"You know what?" he said. "I think you're probably right." Then to himself, but it is my business. It's my friend and my messages too.

The day was drawing on, the sunshine had gone and Adrian was in Dorking, crossing the busy A24 and wandering down a footpath towards the River Mole. The road continued through commuterland, with these strange moments for the river crossings in each valley. Here it was great tree trunks to leap across all the way to dry land on the other side. It was all rather charming. Why was a government department celebrating Guy Fawkes? Perhaps they all did in decades gone by, when November 5th was a really big deal, as it had been in his childhood.

He imagined putting in for some kind of Treasury subvention for rockets and Catherine wheels these days and grinned at the insanity of it. He would never be able to show his face again in the Treasury canteen, where the elite of the nation's thirty-seven year-olds rubbed shoulders with each other at lunchtime. Fireworks? Are you insane? We're not even allowed biscuits for our internal meetings...

Then it struck him. Catherine wheels. The lady of the wheel. Had he not passed some ancient crumbling structure called – yes it was, St Catherine's? He hadn't really looked at it properly. He had just swanned on past like so many pilgrims on the Old Road, though clearly St Catherine's Chapel had attracted many of them. There was a pattern on the road, it was becoming clear. It carried on along the southern slopes of the hill and, every so often, there would be a place of pilgrimage or rest, or some combination of the two, on a little detour to the south. That was St Catherine's Chapel.

There was a railway station back the way he had come on the A24. He skipped back across the river to the main road. There was Dorking station and, when he reached it, there was a train indicated to

Guildford. His luck was in.

The chapel was even more dilapidated than he expected. He had wasted no time. Tall rusty railings surrounded the ruin, with clumps of grass growing out of the medieval masonry, but the light was also beginning to fade, there was nobody around at all. Where should he start? Peter would hardly have left the clue outside the structure, but how was he to get in?

It only took a few minutes to find a spot where the railings had been broken and rusted away. Even Peter, nearly eighty, would have found no difficulty negotiating that one, and neither – judging by the footprints – had anyone else. But even inside the bare stone structure, where once the medieval paintings would have lit up the walls in blues and browns and reds, he felt no better off. Where would you go, given that there were niches in the walls capable of holding one of Peter's clues every few inches?

Come on, what would Peter do? How would Peter think? By the high altar, or where it had once stood? He looked around dead centre by the eastern end. Nothing there, but he had given it only a cursory look. Then he looked around and suddenly it was obvious. What was it Peter had always said about the Pilgrim's Way? He had repeated it over and over again, and Hilaire Belloc seemed to have come up with the insight first. Adrian took off his jacket and rootled around in his rucksack. He knew he had marked a spot and turned down the corner of the page, in a way Peter would never have approved. The book fell open and he read:

> "We know that in every case where the Old Road passes directly past a village church, it passes to the south. From the south, as we have already seen, the entry of the traveller was made; for, to repeat the matter, a custom presumably much older than our religion, gave approach to sacred places from the side of the sun."

There was something special about the south, the side of the sun, that medieval churches always seemed to have their entrances that side. Perhaps it was a pagan memory, he wondered? Even as he searched around for the old door on the southern side, Adrian could see something white in the lintel. He raced over the parched and exhausted flagstones. He had to reach a little and it fell into his hands, another plastic tube like the one used in Alresford, and inside there was another note, written much more carefully and calmly. Peter was clearly not so nervous at this stage. He unfolded it, and his hands shook. As he did so, his mobile phone vibrated in his pocket.

"Barley! How lovely to hear you!" Don't overdo it, Adrian, he told himself.

"Listen, Adrian. You've got to be careful."

"I am being careful. Guess what, Barley. You'll never guess where..."

"Adrian, I've had my house turned over. Someone broke in and turned it upside down."

"What! Are you alright?"

"Oh yes," she said blithely. "I'm fine. There's actually nothing taken, at least I don't think so, and the children weren't there, thank God. It's just a terrible mess. Clothes everywhere, bookcases turned over. It was almost as if they were looking for something. They didn't bother with my credit cards or computer."

"Well, it does happen from time to time..." Adrian wasn't sure what to say.

"But I didn't really connect it with you, except that I've just heard – the pub we went to was also broken into last night." A cold shiver ran down Adrian's spine. Clearly his conspiracy theories were closer to the truth than he had realised.

VII

"We so halted and watched till darkness had completely fallen; then we turned down northward to Alresford to sleep, and next morning before daybreak, when we had satisfied the police who had arrested us upon suspicion of I know not what crime, we took the hill again and rejoined the Old Road."
Hilaire Belloc, *The Old Road*, page 134.

Adrian sat with his muddy rucksack between his knees amidst the commuters on the train speeding into London Waterloo. The trouser legs were covered in dust and dried mud stuck to the walking shoes that seemed to have been superglued to his feet. He felt very out of place and self-conscious, dressed so differently from everyone else with that smug sense of popping up to London for a summer evening on the South Bank. Old copies of the *Evening Standard* from the outward journey were still scuffing along the floor.

He looked around nervously. Nobody seemed to

106

be paying him any attention; nobody was glancing in his direction. So, very gingerly, he reached inside his jacket pocket, unzipped the place where he kept his wallet, and pulled out the latest clue:

"Cavell, Evans and Barley's daughter;
It's a long way down to fetch the water."

He fingered it as if the creased and slightly muddy paper was a last link to Peter, as in a way indeed it was. There was a playfulness about this clue which the others had lacked. It was written relatively neatly, with a biro rather than the stub of a broken pencil. Clearly, Peter had intended the trip mainly as a game at this stage on his trip to Winchester. Perhaps he was unsure whether to take the threat seriously or not.

It struck Adrian, for the first time, that he was in a similar situation – unsure whether to take the forces ranged against him seriously. Unsure even whether they were a figment of his imagination, when everything in his civil service training conspired to persuade him to dismiss the whole caboodle as conspiracy theorising.

Peter had clearly felt something along the same lines too, at least when he wrote this clue. But now he was dead. It makes a fellow think, said Adrian grinning to himself. Then he stopped grinning and remembered his determination; he was being followed, his footsteps were dogged. There had been three break-ins at linked addresses within the last thirty-six hours. Something was wrong and the initials ODF seemed to lie at the bottom of it.

It also occurred to him as strange that Peter should have used Barley's daughter in the clue when, as he must have known, Adrian had not seen her for years – was not even aware that she had children, let alone a daughter. What was she called again?

He ran through his mind all the acronyms, or possible acronyms, he could think of – Open Document Format? Own Damn Fault? Hardly... Oregon Department of Forestry – well, it seemed unlikely that this body would have any interest in these strange pieces of paper he was carrying around. Certainly not to scare an old man like Peter Shilling to death for them. But it was now time to find out. He would go home, fetch his government pass and go straight to the National Archives and check it out. It might not be online in their catalogue – Barley had told him she had tried – but there would be some giveaway in a dusty old civil service directory long forgotten somewhere. There was bound to be.

Office of the Procurator Fiscal? Too Scottish, and

the wrong letter anyway. Organisation of Dental Finance? Hardly; was there any such august body? As he walked down the familiar suburban streets to his home, he began to relax again and convince himself that there really was nothing to worry about. Then he reached the middle of his own road. Opposite his front door, by the dustbins and recycling boxes, a man was smoking. He seemed familiar for some reason, his face was pasty white and he had a small, grey beard. He was watchful, staring half expectantly in the other direction. Then looking back vaguely in his direction. Next to him was a white van.

Adrian stopped. He was about a hundred yards away still and may not be obvious, but he was aware he must not make a sudden change of direction. He bent down to do up his shoelace and looked furtively over to the man again. He was looking directly at him.

Adrian straightened up, looked theatrically in his pockets as if he had forgotten his front door key, turned around and walked briskly away. Behind him, he heard an engine starting and dodged quickly down the alleyway, past the rubbish, and hid behind a large grey wheelie bin. Nothing went by, then a scooter. Could that have been it, or was the white van waiting for him? Just to make sure, he ran quickly to the other end of the lane, into the recreation ground and jumped over what had once been a healthy looking stream but was now filled with empty Lucozade bottles. Then, carrying his rucksack, he scrambled up into another alleyway and found himself back by the same suburban station he had left a quarter of an hour before.

He glanced both ways up the road. No white vans. Then he heard the unmistakable noise of the Victoria train approaching, with the tingling of the rails and a small hopeful dot in the distance. He made a dash for it, through the barriers and up the slope onto the platform. A moment later he was shaking his way into back into London.

It was clear he couldn't go home, at least not now. But never mind – he didn't really need his pass. He had his driving licence and probably, among the pieces of paper stashed alongside his toothbrush and other items, there would be a household bill because he had picked up a pile of unopened post when he left home originally. He would simply apply for a reader's pass when he got to the National Archives at Kew. He had done it before; there was really no reason why he shouldn't do it again.

It was only then, relaxing as the old chimney pots swept past the train window, that he remembered the name of Barley's daughter. It was Edith.

With his new pass in his back pocket, Adrian sat at a terminal in the National Archives and looked around at the elderly gents doing their military genealogies and the young Ph.D. students taking photographic documents, and the sunshine across Kew wafting in through the window. What an extraordinary place it was, like a small city dedicated to the paperwork of the past.

He was waiting for the telltale signalling system to inform him that his documents were ready for him, and congratulating himself for escaping such close pursuit. He had found that Nadia had been completely correct: there was no listing for ODF in the computer indexing system, but he had called up three civil service directories – 1867, 1908 and 1957 – in the hope that there would be some listing.

He spent his time, after a quick cup of tea in the cafe, wondering about the significance of Edith. Edith Cavell, the martyred nurse, that was easy enough. So was Dame Edith Evans and Barley's daughter too. The first line was evidently designed to mean Edith, but what was the reference to water about? Edith's Lake, River Edith, Lake Edith? That wasn't clear, but perhaps it would be once he got onto the Old Road again.

The light flashed. He went to his little box where they were supposed to be delivered. It didn't look as if anyone had asked to see these directories since they were heaved out of Whitehall and deposited with the archives. The 1957 edition had a bus ticket in it. It said 2d. There was no ODF in the index and no likely organisations with initials in the least bit like that. He turned to 1867. Typical, no index – how were the civil servants under Gladstone supposed to look things up? He reached for the 1908 edition, beginning to kick himself for a wasted journey – where else could he look? Perhaps he was looking too far back. He would try in the 1980s. As he opened the book, there was a tap on his shoulder.

"Excuse me, sir, there's a gentleman who says he has to talk to you rather urgently. He has no pass, so I asked him to wait by the barrier. Adrian glanced over at a man staring at him from the distance in a strange overcoat. He looked like a policeman.

Perhaps this was the moment to talk to them, he wondered – in the open where they can't hit me over the head or give me a truth serum or lethal injection or whatever these lunatics wanted to do. They can't bundle me into a fast car when I'm in the National Archives. You can't bundle anything into anything here.

"Thank you," he said. "Tell him I'm on my way and will just put these back into the box."

He picked up the three directories. They weighed

unexpectedly heavy as he carried them all back to the counter in their folder. As he did so, he reached into his inside pocket and drew out the clues. Just to make sure. They were there. The policeman could hardly see accurately at this angle. Adrian slipped them into the pages of 1908, shut the book and handed it back over the desk. At least he would know where they were if he ever needed them again. Nobody else ever seemed to look there.

He took a deep breath, remembering he was a senior member of staff at the Treasury. This was not a moment to feel cowed by a policeman, however mysterious. Then he strode out, fixing the man with the confident stare of a Whitehall mandarin.

"I am sorry to take so long," he smiled.

"Mr Matinson? I apologise for intruding at this time. John Hammond, Special Branch. I need to ask you one or two questions." He flashed an ID card.

"Oh yes, what about?"

"Well, perhaps I could explain on the way."

Adrian looked a little less confident. "On the way where? I don't really have time to go with you anywhere."

"Well, sir," said Hammond, taking a deep breath. "If you wouldn't mind coming with me to my office, about half an hour away. I'd be happy to bring you back here or take you where you'd like to go next."

This seemed like a reasonable man. Could he trust him? Adrian wasn't sure. Then he thought of the thug with a beard who he had seen smoking outside his home and he knew which one he preferred to deal with. In Nazi war films there was always one of the Gestapo who would offer you a cigarette. It made sense to latch onto that one, given the choice.

"Alright, I accept – on condition that you will also answer some of *my* questions."

The policeman looked a little put out. "I may not be able to. As long as you understand that?"

"Where is your office exactly?" Adrian had assumed they would be going into central London. In fact, they appeared to be heading west along the M4. The traffic was as heavy as it usually was, pumping noxious fumes into the atmosphere. He attempted to engage Mr Hammond in conversation, with little success and had relaxed, his eyelids drooping, as they sped out of London.

"Oh, Heathrow. Only a jiffy."

After a quick dive through a security gate, Adrian was ushered into a non-descript concrete building and his Special Branch minder led him into an interview room. They sat silently opposite each other.

"So? What do you want to know?" asked Adrian, trying to break the silence.

"Sorry, sir. Just waiting for my boss."

"Oh," said Adrian, a little nettled. "I had assumed you'd be doing the interview yourself." He was beginning to regret his decision to come when there was a step outside the room and a flurry of papers, and the boss swept into the room. She was attractive and somewhat fierce looking. There were no pleasantries. She read the file in front of her, which looked remarkably thin, with an air of increasing concern.

"Mr Matinson? My name is Susan Letcher. I'm the superintendent for this district. I'm grateful to you for helping us. I understand that you are in the possession of some pieces of paper which I have been asked to recover. Messages, I believe, from a friend of yours, Dr Peter Shilling?"

"Are you telling me or asking me?"

"My understanding is that you have these papers and I have been asked, on the highest authority, to request that you pass them on to us."

"You understand wrong, I'm afraid."

Susan Letcher looked up sharply and quizzically. "May I ask where they are?"

"You certainly may, but you will have to explain your interest in what are basically notes written by a friend to me and really of no possible interest to anyone else."

Ms Letcher studied the file again; then she shut it.

"I'm sorry. I'm not at liberty to say. And, of course, you are at liberty not to answer my questions. It's my task to persuade you that it would be better for everyone involved if you assisted us on this."

"Including me?"

"Definitely including you."

Adrian considered. There was no point in making enemies. It may be that he would need all the friends he could get.

"No, I'm happy to help as much as I can, but I threw them away. They were just a game he was playing with me. I have... had... known him for many years, you understand. I will have to ask you again what your interest is in them. They really were just scraps of paper."

"I'm sorry, Mr Matinson, but we're not at liberty to divulge."

Adrian could feel his irritation rising again. "Well, I'm sorry, but if you're not at liberty to divulge your reasons for questioning me, then I'm not sure I'm at liberty to help you further." He crossed his arms.

The superintendent stared at the file in front of her. It occurred to Adrian suddenly that she was uncomfortable. She gave Hammond a barely perceptible nod and they both stood up. "Excuse me a moment," she said. "I'm just going to consult with my colleague outside."

A moment later, Adrian was alone in the room. How many criminals had sat and sweated in here? Probably illegal immigrants too, he suggested to himself, and why on earth should Special Branch be involved with him when he knew perfectly well they were involved with political crime. What was their interest in Peter's death? He would ask the moment they came back in.

A few minutes later, the door opened. In came Hammond, the man he had met at Kew. There was no sign of Superintendent Letcher. He sat down.

"Mr Matinson, I'm afraid you'll have to forgive us." He looked uncomfortable. "My boss has authorised me to tell you as much as we know, which, as you'll hear, is not very much. We have been asked to contact you and ask about the whereabouts of the papers by a government department – in this case the Home Office, but they are actually acting on behalf of another agency and I'm afraid we are not at liberty to disclose which one. All we know is that we were asked to ask you the question. We've done that, and perhaps I might supplement it by asking *where* you disposed of them and when?"

"Ah well, I chucked them out as they came in,

really. Just put them in the bin."

"May I ask which bin?"

"The bin wherever I was staying at the time. I can give you a list if that would help? All before I reached Farnham."

Hammond looked up suddenly. "But my understanding is that you came into possession of another one in Farnham?"

"So you do know more than that. I'll tell you it all, I'm being as honest as I can. Yes, I disposed of them and yes, there was another one I was given in Farnham and I threw it straight away there and then. It was only a scrubby bit of paper. I think I put it on the fire."

"There was a fire? In May?"

"Actually, yes." Hammond wrote doggedly. "Now can I ask you a question?"

"You can try."

"Why are you interested?"

"Well, as I explained, Mr Matinson, we're not in fact interested ourselves. We are acting on information and a request from another department."

"So you don't know why you've brought me here?"

"Beyond what I've said already? Yes, well, it is probably fair to say we don't know precisely the reason we were approached..."

"So why am I being followed?"

Hammond breathed a sigh. "In my experience, people who say they are being followed are usually either very tired or suffering from delusions of grandeur. I expect you're just very tired. I hope you don't mind me suggesting that I think the best thing would be to have a very good night's sleep. Now, if there's nothing else, I'm happy to fulfil our agreement by ordering you a car to wherever you want to go."

"So you don't actually know any more than me. You know less than me, in fact. Is that right?" Hammond ignored this.

"Can you confirm that you're not following me?"

Hammond glanced again at the file, as if it might enlighten him.

"What I can say is that, to the very best of my knowledge, we are not having you followed. I can say that. Now, where would you like to be taken?"

"Oh, Euston station, if you don't mind."

Twelve hours later, Adrian heaved on his rucksack again, tied up his walking boots and set off for a second time across the tree stump bridge over the River Mole and on up the foothills of Box Hill. The day was bright and calm and, for the first time, he was looking forward to enjoying the Pilgrim's Way.

He had not stayed long in Euston Station. Just long enough to queue up for a ticket at the counter and get through the barrier, before doubling back five minutes later and down the underground to Waterloo, then catching a train back to Dorking. He was suddenly determined to follow Peter's clues no matter where they might lead, and to do so as quickly as possible before there were any more interventions. It was the surest way he could think of for finding the truth. So, with the woods above him, the ancient yews that marked the route of the Old Road etched out against the sky, he headed into the North Downs.

Adrian trudged on. It was almost hypnotic as he put one foot in front of the other. He marvelled how the human frame could stand it, one leg, the other leg, for hour after hour, with a few minutes snatched here and there for a drink or a sandwich in a pub. As he came nearer the top of Box Hill, he began worrying about the police and the white van and everything else, but he soon found his mind meandering onto more mundane matters – like his kitchen, his job, Nadia and Barley.

Barley popped into his head too much for

comfort. He suppressed her, unsure what aspect of her to think about, but she would keep wheedling her way in.

The air was bracing, the tracks were becoming easier to follow, though he occasionally found himself lost in a ploughed field before glimpsing the telltale line of yews. But all around him, too, were examples of agriculture driven out over the centuries by property and horses and the vulgar speculations of stockbrokers. There were muddy tracks over the chalk and stringy remains of ancient woods past the hideous modern gates, more Range Rovers in the drive and pompous statues of lions at bay.

There were the unmistakable signs of the nouveau riche at play, the tennis courts and the abandoned fields full of melons or pumpkins, lost to whatever speculation in foodstuffs had brought the price of production above the sale price.

There were also those concrete and encrusted, broken old defence installations, the pillboxes and forgotten Observer Corps emplacements, ready to defend London in 1940 should they need to. It was almost as if it was the Old Road itself which had been defended, were it not for the fact that so much of it had been sold off.

All these huge houses, built on the foundations of religious establishments or hostels for pilgrims, or hospitals run by monks, sold off to friends of the court of Henry VIII. Time after time, Adrian found himself staring again as the Old Road strode out down some gravel drive which sang the song of 'Private Property', and which prevented him from following the exact line of the Way. Anything religious, and it had been appropriated by the up-and-coming lords of Protestantism.

Still, it was gentle walking for the next three days, as Adrian slid effortlessly past the tennis courts and ancient quarries – the one at Merstham had once supplied the stone for Westminster Abbey and Windsor Castle, or so his guide book told him – before dipping down into some modern road or railway cutting.

Sometimes the road was almost washed away in the middle of puny remains of a wood filled with old mattresses and the detritus of sleeping out, or dumped kitchen equipment – the remains of some extreme marital tiff – strewn over the mound that marked the medieval edge of the road. Sometimes it rejoined the tarmacked reality with official signs recognising it as 'Pilgrim's Way'.

As he walked, Adrian began by agonising about Peter and the police, and the white van, though soon the liberating monotony of walking calmed his mind and that began to meander more gently too, about his job. Or Barley's children. He thought of her increasingly, wondering what she was doing, and whether she had recovered properly from the break-in, and whether the burglars would come back. He was constantly tempted to call her but he stopped still, staring out over the fields to the M25 or the weald of Kent, or the Foreign Secretary's official residence at Chevening, and managed to prevent himself.

She would be disturbed if he rang so soon. He didn't want to plague her, did he...?

As his mind wandered along with his feet, he occasionally found himself returning to his immediate conundrum. The question about River Edith. Where was it? There had been no sign of it by the time he reached Otford and relaxed finally in front of the facade of the Archbishop's Palace.

This was supposed to be Becket's birthplace, though clearly these ruins were built some centuries after Becket. It reminded Adrian that this was, in a sense, the place which had started it all. By giving birth to Thomas Becket, Otford had truly started the ball rolling. It had, after all, been the murder of Becket, when Archbishop of Canterbury in 1170 – by four knights believing that they were carrying out the orders of the king – which had first set pilgrims travelling down the Old Road. Though, as Peter was always telling him, it was considerably older than that.

In fact, the repetitive placing of one foot in front of the other, and the increasing awareness of his small rucksack on his back, as he hitched the weight from shoulder to shoulder, had been enough to awaken some fellow feeling between Adrian and the pilgrims who had gone before them. He had appreciated their stories before – he had studied Chaucer at university – but he had never quite been able to imagine them trudging every step of the way, day after exhausting day. Through the mud and the rain – or, then again, through the dust and the heat.

What kind of society was it, he wondered, that would make people sacrifice a week of their lives in this way to pay tribute at Becket's tomb, and to do so with at least some reverence and piety? Perhaps in some ways it was obvious: it was the society where the ability of the church to stand up to temporal power, in the name of ordinary people, was valued enough to make it worth a pilgrimage.

It is a pity no such power existed now, Adrian thought to himself, before realising what a heresy this was: he was a civil servant at the Treasury. His Treasury colleagues wanted no such balance of powers if they could possibly help it. No such intervention by the lords spiritual in the worldly decisions his colleagues had to take.

What if someone was thinking of relaunching the pilgrimage – to assert the power of conscience against government – that would certainly ruffle a few feathers among his senior colleagues. He wondered vaguely whether anyone had actually tried. Still, it wouldn't be exactly easy; Becket had been dead more than eight centuries, and his bones had disappeared before the arrival of Henry VIII's commissioners at Canterbury. They were in time to remove the precious stones from the casket and tomb, but the bones had gone and have never turned up since. Their resting place had long since been forgotten, if indeed they did rest and had not been turned into dust or ashes like those of the Norman kings at the hands of the French revolutionaries.

He found a pub for lunch and began to unwind. He had reached Kent and walked what seemed like twenty or thirty miles in a couple of days, and though he was no nearer finding Edith's water, he felt a strong sense of accomplishment. Peter Shilling had clearly left him this legacy and he very much appreciated it.

Even so, perhaps it was finally time to turn his mobile phone back on. There were a number of missed calls and two messages. One was from Nadia asking where he was. Some official had been looking for him in the office. The other was evidently from Barley. Adrian found his heart leaping with excitement. He criticised himself for feeling that strange levity and suppressed it.

Yet he called her straight back. The sunshine was on his face and the facade of the Archbishop's ruined palace looked strangely as if it had only just been abandoned.

"Adrian!"

"Hello – how are you? I got your call."

"Yes, I'm well…" The conversation appeared to be struggling already, as if Barley didn't want to talk about any of the mundane things of life either, but neither of them could think of anything else to say. "How are you getting on? It must be tough. Where have you got to so far?"

"Ah well, I've got blisters if that's what you mean. I've got as far as – well, hold on I've promised myself not to say where I am over the phone. Just in case." He probably sounded paranoid. There was a silence at the other end of the phone. Really, he couldn't pretend he knew her any more than he ever had, and in retrospect that wasn't terribly well.

126

"No, you're right, Adrian. I've been worrying about you. The thing is, I've remembered something that Peter said when we met and it might just have a bearing on all this."

"Oh yes?"

"But the thing is that I agree with you about using the phone – just in case, as you say. Listen, my ex is taking the children for the next couple of days. They're practicing for sailing his yacht to France in a week or so. He always has them Thursdays and Fridays and then the weekend when it's his turn, which isn't terribly often actually. Why don't I come and meet you?"

Adrian rocked on his heels. "Really? That would be absolutely brilliant." Steady on, he told himself.
"But I've been wondering how we can arrange to meet without naming a place."

"OK, how about this?" said Adrian, unfolding his map on his knee. "You know where I'm going and vaguely where I am. I'm looking at a big river coming up tomorrow, in about ten miles. Where my path meets the river – there must be a bridge – I'll meet you there. How about that? Does that make any sense?"

"Hold on. OK, I'm looking at the map. So we're not talking about a river beginning with D then, you could be there?"

"No, no, somewhere more in the middle of the alphabet." How could he tell her without using the word 'Medway'? "Oh and one other thing, don't forget to put your shed away..."

There was another silence. "My shed? Oh, I see, yes!" She laughed. "Very good, Adrian. Yes, I'm putting it away now, as we speak." She laughed again. It was fun playing at spies. And the thugs seemed a long way away now.

"What time?"

"Well, I reckon I could be there by noon tomorrow, say?"

VIII

*"These seven converging lines of proof, or rather of
suggestion – seven points which ingenuity or
research might easily develop into a greater
number – seem to me to settle the discussion in
favour of Snodland."*
Hilaire Belloc, *The Old Road*, pages 252-3.

Adrian stared at the river as it moved inexorably
towards the North Sea, carrying the detritus of a
rainy summer, chunks of riverbank, more Lucozade
bottles, bits of painted wood. It was too wide to cross
and too powerful to swim against, with its cold,
chalky colour. He looked at his watch. It was still
only 11.30, but he had been walking for four hours
since staying the night in Kemsing. There was also
clearly a problem he would have to solve somehow.
He had asked Barley to meet him by the bridge, but
there was no bridge.

He had been so sure there would be a bridge to
cross the Medway at Snodland but, as far as he could
tell, there was nothing of the kind anywhere nearby.

Even in Belloc's day there had been a small ferry. How could he have agreed to meet Barley by a clearly non-existent bridge? There was a battered medieval church and a large paper factory, but otherwise the road petered out. He stood by the side of the river and stared across. It was frustrating. In the distance, on the shingle, there was some old footwear, not in pairs, some muddy buckets and an old rowing boat with water in the bottom, drawn up out of the flow of the current. It was tempting but insane. In any case, he could hardly take Barley across on such a risky mode of transport.

In his pocket, he fingered the next clue and congratulated himself for finally tracking down St Edith's Well, for that was what it had turned out to be. It had been at Kemsing and as soon as he had seen a sign to it he had realised that was where he was intended to go. He had taken the path down from the main road, which the Pilgrim's Way became before Otford, until he had stood opposite the enormous old well, retired of recent years – but not restored so much that Peter had been unable to shove another of his plastic tubes into the brickwork.

Adrian had found it almost immediately and, checking first over his shoulder, had taken it out and read it. This is what it said:

"Of the lost prince who could be king,
And gave it all up to do the mason's thing."

He puzzled again for a moment, wondering if he could think of any kings or princes who had been prominent Freemasons. Wasn't there something about the Duke of Kent? Perhaps he was a little too modern for Peter Shilling. He would ask Barley when she arrived. He remembered her mind was almost as stocked with irrelevant historical tittle-tattle as Peter's had been.

Twenty minutes to go. He turned round and headed off back towards the crumbling shopping centre and its dull round of fried chicken enclaves and charity shops, with the occasional barred off-licence, which made up the high street. He realised as he did so that he did not know what kind of car to expect her to arrive in.

Where was she now? Probably passing through Otford, as he had done himself just a couple of days before. Adrian ambled slowly past a rundown supermarket, one door barricaded with cardboard boxes. A drunk was outside clutching a can of lager. Perhaps the Pilgrimage had actually been more like this than the way Chaucer had portrayed it. Chaucer's Canterbury Tales had included a drunken bawdiness in many of his stories. But then – he reminded himself – that was on the Pilgrim's Way out of London; not such an ancient track as this one.

He had a cup of tea in a greasy spoon, read a newspaper and ambled back to the river in time to meet Barley. He felt strangely elated as if this was some kind of date, which he constantly reminded himself that it was not. He speculated also about what Peter may have said to her, maybe there was some explanation for the clues and the skulduggery. Maybe there was even some reasonable explanation for the thugs who appeared to have turned their attention to him.

Were they thugs, he mused? He had yet to meet and talk to one of them except, of course, the man he met on his own stairs, and – let's be fair – that was rather an unexpected conjunction on both sides. Neither of them had been entirely prepared or on their best behaviour.

For the second time that morning, he stared down at the great light-brown river swirling around the bend and imagined the pilgrims queuing up for the ferryman, backwards and forwards. Then he turned around and, in the distance, there she was. He hailed her and walked briskly towards her.

"Barley! Thanks so much for coming."

"Nonsense. Wouldn't have missed it for the world. An adventure. And I want to know what Peter was driving at as much as you do." She smiled at him.

Faintly disappointed that there was some practical reason for seeing him, Adrian avoided her gaze for a moment.

"Still. It's lovely to see you," he said.

Barley seemed barely to acknowledge this statement. She was staring back behind her.

Adrian followed her gaze. A familiar white van was driving slowly towards them, past the end of the shopping precinct.

"You gathered that there's no bridge," he said.

"I realised that when I tried to park a few minutes ago. Look – that's the van, isn't it? The one you keep talking about?"

With a horrible dip in the pit of his stomach, Adrian realised it was. "I don't really like the look of this. Come on, let's walk a bit faster. They must have been listening in to our conversation. So much for my clever code."

The river swirled ahead of them. There really was no crossing that way. To the right, the paper plant with high wire fences. To the left, there was the old churchyard and then what looked like people's back gardens. Adrian glanced round. The van was approaching towards them, and it was a dead end. There was no way back.

"Can you jump down with me?"

"Not sure." Barley looked nervously down at the muddy shingle.

"I'm not sure we've got any alternative."

He scrambled down the bank and held out a hand to her. She looked down and leapt, and sank an inch or so into the mud.

"You're not planning to swim for it?"

"I don't think we'd make it," he said, reassuringly. "But there's an old boat."

The mud was a little fresher around the bend in the river and nearly over their shoes. They skipped from stone to stone. Now they were a little closer, the boat didn't seem quite as seaworthy as it had from the bank.

There was the sound of a van door being banged shut and, a moment later, the man's head loomed over the top of the riverbank where they had been. He shouted something. He didn't seem friendly.

"Come on. There it is."

"What's he shouting?"

"Not sure. Was it 'Come here you runts'?"

"It's full of water, Adrian!"

"Come on, lift this side and I think it will float."

The water poured back from whence it came.

"Don't think about it."

Barley was giggling now. She seemed to be enjoying it for some reason. Together they pushed the boat backwards into the water. It wobbled. Adrian held it still and Barley leapt in.

"This is completely crazy," she said. There was a nervous moment as Adrian threw in his backpack, waded into the mud and jumped into the boat. It powered backwards into the stream, wobbling terrifyingly.

"We're just living to fight another day." He mumbled breathlessly, finding the centre of balance.

"What about an oar?" shouted Barley.

He hadn't thought of that, but there was an old branch back on the bank. There wasn't much time. The two men were climbing down the bank just downstream. They had maybe fifteen seconds. Adrian reached for the end of the branch under water. Barley leaned the other way and used it to push off.

The boat now spun around in the current. Adrian broke the branch in two with a deft movement born of panic and handed Barley the other half.

"Come on. Paddle!"

They paddled like mad and the boat swung over towards the next bend. From behind, Adrian could hear men swearing at them from the other bank. What did they actually want? The boat seemed to be going too fast.

To their great relief, the bend shifted them

towards the opposite bank and there was another branch leaning across the river on the right. It looked dead and waterlogged.

"Come on!" shouted Adrian. "Over there!" There was a great deal of splashing and Adrian felt the water going up his sleeves and down his trousers.

"Quick! Grab it!" said Barley as the branch came towards them.

Adrian grabbed and, for a moment, it seemed as if the boat would tip but instead, at the last second, it swung over into an eddy.

"I'm going to have to jump in, aren't I?" he said reluctantly.

"You're such a gentleman," she laughed.

A moment later, he was up to his thighs, hauling the boat onto the gravel. They climbed out, puffing heavily, hauled out Adrian's rucksack and fell into the grass above the bank, laughing. He peeped over the tufts of grass that hid them, now they were high on the bank again they could just see round the bend, and there were the two men in shirtsleeves staring downstream. One was on his mobile phone, gesticulating in the direction of the river.

"Have you got a map?" she asked. "You realise my car's on the other side?"

"I know, and there's no way across for five miles. Aylesford, I think. Or the M2."

"Let's get to the nearest pub and call a cab," she said.

"Bonnie Prince Charlie? Wasn't he a lost prince who could be king?" said Barley. They were in the Windmill on the Rochester Road in Burham and discussing the latest clue. Adrian was eating a packet of ready salted crisps.

"That was Scotland, and it was 1745 or 1746 or something. We need medieval England. Don't we?" he added, nervous that he had been too dismissive.

She went back to staring out of the window. It isn't often you are chased into a river by two men and a van and the hilarity had worn off. Adrian felt calm and satisfied with life. He wasn't sure if she did.

"Look, Barley – it's lovely of you to come down and meet me like this but how am I going to get you home – at least back to your car?"

"Really, I wouldn't have missed the boat trip for anything. You really know how to give a girl a good time."

They both laughed.

"No, look, Adrian," she said, suddenly serious. "I'm actually rather worried about you. Those men meant business, though I've no idea what it was. And the reason I wanted to come was that I've remembered what Peter said. He said he'd made a breakthrough."

"A breakthrough? What did he mean?"

"Well, obviously, I asked him, and he said he didn't want to say quite yet but that – if anything happened to him..."

"He really said that?"

"Yes, what with everything that has happened, I'd forgotten our conversation. He said, if anything happened to him, he'd left some pointers to you – 'pointers', that's what he called them – so that you would know."

Adrian took a deep breath. Then he was afraid of something. He had been right to have these niggles about Peter's death. There *was* something going on.

"You know, Barley, it's rather a relief to hear that. I've had such a civil service training that I'm constantly checking myself to avoid anything that smacks of conspiracy theory. But there is something going on. You can't avoid the evidence, can you?" It was a rhetorical question. "I suppose those 'pointers' are the bits of paper I've been following. Perhaps that's why there's been such interest in them. And I don't like the look of those men either. What would have happened if they'd caught us, do you think?"

"I don't know. I don't know. I'm worried about you, Adrian, and I'd like to make a suggestion. So hear me out." Adrian sat back expectant.

"Go ahead then. I'm not going to stop you."

"Look. They must know, now, that you're on the Pilgrim's Way. That means all they have to do is wait for you. They look pretty stupid, I know, but they're not so stupid that they can't look at an old map. I suggest you come back to London with me tonight; I'll drive you. And then you can get some protection – I mean you work for the government, don't you? You must know some powerful people; I think you should take them into your confidence and ask them to find out what's going on."

"Just as long as this isn't actually the government I'm up against."

"I thought you didn't do conspiracy theories? In any case – those two bruisers who swore so violently at us when we were risking our lives in that leaky boat. Not really government material, were they – not exactly James Bond?"

"OK, next question. How do we get back across the river?"

"I thought we were going to get a cab. Simple. We can't be that far from a river crossing."

Adrian thought for a moment in silence. "I'm not going to abandon Peter's clues, if that's what you mean. Especially as I've just guessed what the next one must refer to…"

"I've guessed too. The Princes in the Tower."

"Of course it is – I'm just not sure what the link is with the Pilgrim's Way."

"We'll come back here, alright Adrian? I'll come with you. Just let's get out of here for now. Come on, let's order a cab."

"You know," said Barley, as they hurtled back down the narrow roads to the unprepossessing, peeling shopping street in Snodland where her car was parked, "I know exactly what Peter meant by that clue."

"The one about the princes?"

"Hold on, it's the news." She leant over and asked the cab driver to turn up the radio.

It was the referendum again. "The prime minister has hit back at accusations from his own colleagues that he is losing control of cabinet unity," said the radio,

"Oh, that old stuff again. You know what's really going on, don't you, Adrian?"

"No, I only work at the Treasury. Nobody tells us anything."

"It's a coup, that's what it is," she said with a kind of flourish. "Two leading members of the cabinet are trying to take over the country."

"You might be right."

"And what I want to know is, how much the civil service are helping them."

"Helping them? I don't know anyone in the civil service who doesn't regard them as head-bangers."

Barley leant over and talked more quietly. "You know Peter thought they were getting high-placed backing."

Peter's heart sank. Not another conspiracy theory? The Queen? Prince Philip...?

"But then it isn't really his era is it?"

"What?"

"Sorry, I was thinking about Prince Philip."

Barley looked at him oddly and ignored it. "You see, Peter took me aside as he left the pub. Just took me to the door and said: 'Mark my words, Barley. They're all in it together.'"

"I say again – who?"

"That's what I said. Then he said something a bit odd – he said: 'You know – the people who burned Guy Fawkes.'"

"Is that what you wanted to tell me?"

"No," said Barley, with a meaningful face and, nodding at the driver, whispered, "I'll tell you when we get to Snodland. Oh, I know what I wanted to say. Knowing Peter, it *had* to be the Princes in the Tower. Didn't it?"

It was true that Peter Shilling was obsessed with the Princes in the Tower, and Adrian knew this. Barley had to be right. He was obsessed with the idea that one at least of them had actually escaped, and lived on.

"You're probably right. But what have the Princes in the Tower got to do with the Pilgrim's Way?"

"I don't know, Adrian. That's why you're walking it, isn't it?"

"Well, I'm not walking it now, am I? I've just agreed to nip back to London with you."

He was aware suddenly that this didn't sound quite as friendly as he might have meant. "I mean, it's lovely to see more of you Barley."

It was indeed, he mused. How often had he longed to share a cab with Barley in days gone by when he had worn flared trousers? Perhaps, in retrospect, it had been the flared trousers, rather than any shortcomings in himself, which had led to his failure to win her erotic interest. But then again, the flared trousers may just have represented a shortcoming in him.

"Somewhere along here, there's something to do with the Princes. That's all I suggest," said Barley, ignoring his sudden silence. "So keep an eye out. We'll both have to keep an eye out."

"We? Are you coming back then?"

"Well, I was thinking of it. This is rather more exciting than life in Darkest Farnham." She sniggered quietly. "But only if you manage to stay out of the clutches of the men in that van."

The taxi dropped them in a housing estate near the car park in Snodland. It was bleak, with old buggies burned out next to the dog shit and piles of broken crockery. They didn't want to march right up to the car. But nobody seemed to be following them.

It was only a few minutes' walk. Adrian felt conspicuous with his rucksack as they edged along the high street. There was Barley's car. They stood and watched. There appeared to be no white vans. Nobody watching.

"OK, let's go then," said Barley. "You stay here. I'll pick you up in a jiffy."

She raced across the tarmac and was in the car with the engine running, pulling away in less than a minute.

"Quick. Rucksack in the back seat. Quick, Adrian."

He had forgotten, over the years, how bossy she was, he thought for a moment, but he did as he was told. A few moments later, they were accelerating out into the main road. Adrian looked anxiously behind but nobody seemed to have followed.

"I don't want to speak too soon, but I have a feeling we got away with that."

"Right now," said Barley, in managerial tone. "Reach into the door next to you. That door there, and then you can get me onto the M26."

They swept through small Kentish villages and commuter-belt towns with large white motors parked up in the driveways. It was England at its least enjoyable. Adrian had been on the Pilgrim's Way now for more than a week and something of it had seeped into his soul. The large cars offended him in ways he could not quite pinpoint.

"Come on then, Barley. What else did Peter say when you met him?"

"Well, there was something – and it was a little odd," she said, changing gear hurriedly to avoid a cyclist. "I thought nothing of it at the time and anyway I don't really understand what he meant, even now. But he said he had also made a discovery."

Adrian's mind reeled. "And?"

"He was a bit cryptic. He said he'd discovered some lost remains. Then we got interrupted by something or other and I forgot about it. He seemed very excited, but obviously careful because he whispered it to me. You know what he was like with his enthusiasms. I never could work out which enthusiasm he was talking about, but the thing is – Adrian, are you listening? – the thing is that he said I must tell you that he would leave some clues in case anything happened. We talked about it in the pub, remember?"

"Like these bits of paper, we agreed... But what's that got to do with his discovery?"

"Well, I obviously didn't ask. Sorry, I wish I had now, clearly." Barley was slightly irritated, you could tell, about this implied criticism.

"I don't know," said Adrian thoughtfully. "Do you think he laid the clues for fun to start with, and then it all started getting a bit serious?"

They were on the motorway now, speeding towards the exit for Croydon and into London. Adrian found himself feeling, almost for the first time since these strange incidents began, content with his life. Here was Barley next to him again after goodness knows how many decades. Yes, Peter was dead, but he had actually enjoyed his health-giving final gift – a week or more on the Pilgrim's Way, walking somehow back to the Middle Ages. He breathed a long sigh.

"You know Barley, I've almost enjoyed all this, now it seems a little less urgent. Not Peter's death of course, but the walking. I don't know if I can face going through with whatever comes next. I'm not sure I was right to come to London."

"Not right? Not see it through? Really?"

She looked suddenly a little dangerous. A distant memory had stirred of some huge argument when they had torn at each other, so many years ago that its origins were now lost.

"Not see it through?" she said again. "You don't think – I don't know – that's a bit the story of your life? Our lives I mean? When did we see things through?"

"Hold on, Barley…"

"I mean, I never see things through. My marriage, my jobs, my plans. And if you'd seen through things with me, just put a bit of staying power in it – I know I'm a sort of flighty and everything – I wouldn't have married that idiot Rob. And *you* wouldn't be a dry old husk who hasn't lived."

"Well…"

Adrian remembered, ever so dimly, previous rants and he kept his mouth firmly closed. Was he really a dry old husk? Why was it he always had to take every insult thrown at him by women and examine it as if it had been intended? Perhaps that was what dry old husks did.

"I mean, don't you think you owe it to Peter to…"

She bit her lip. Small droplets appeared in her eye. "I'm so sorry, Adrian. Please forgive me. That was outrageous and I don't mean any of it."

"What none of it? Even the husk bit? What about the nice bit?"

"What nice bit?"

"The bit about me and you nearly getting together."

"Oh, well…" She grinned and caught his eye momentarily.

"But you're quite right, of course. I will see it through. You'll see."

"Don't for goodness sake stop in Whitehall. You'll get towed away with you still in the car. Drop me in Birdcage Walk or on the bridge," said Adrian. "Listen, Barley, I'm so grateful to you for today. I loved you coming."

She looked at him and then kissed him full on the lips.

He could feel himself responding. Then he briefly kissed her back and was gone.

It took only a few minutes to heave his rucksack onto his back and tidy himself up a little. He remembered there was a shower at the Treasury that he had never used. It might be sensible of him to get a shave somehow too. Then he began to plot his plan of campaign. First stop would be to see his boss, and then have a quick chat with the under-secretary – just to explain the situation. Then catch up with Nadia...

He reached the steps of the Treasury in Whitehall and took his rucksack off, in case he was stopped as a tourist, and held open the door. A man came out as he did so.

"Mr Matinson?"

"Yes."

"Could you come with me a moment, sir? My colleague here will guide you." Adrian was suddenly aware of another man behind him.

"I was just going to my office."

"I'm afraid you will have to come with us now, sir."

Adrian was back in the street. The man in a light raincoat behind him was pressing rather close.

"Well, perhaps I could just..."

"No. Not now, sir. I'm afraid I will have to ask you to come with me. The car is just over here."

He felt the pressure, firmly applied, on his arm.

"I'm not under arrest, am I?"

"I'd prefer not to put it like that, but you will have to come with me. Here is my identification."

Once again, Adrian recognised the official identification card of a member of Special Branch.

IX

"Remote, an Island, impoverished, the first of the frontiers to be abandoned, it was at last overwhelmed: to what extent we can only guess, and in what manner we cannot tell at all, but at any rate with sufficient completeness to make us alone lose the Faith which is the chief bond of civilisation."
Hilaire Belloc, *The Old Road*, page 79.

"Sir Richard will see you now."

Adrian's head swam a little and he steadied himself by looking out of the window at the ancient medieval stone. "Yes, and..." He had been on the verge of saying 'about time too', but realised he was not really in a position to be tetchy. In fact, he was more frightened than angry and he understood that this may be his one opportunity to make some kind of reasonable and dignified exit. He had spent now forty-eight hours in a dire office, painted in the most toxic shade of municipal green, as if he had been locked in a primary school during the days of the London County Council.

He had been brought dinners, teas and coffees on ancient and battered trays, but there had been a plain-clothes policeman, at least there had been every time he looked, stationed outside the door. In practice, he had spent most of his time dozing.

"Am I under arrest?" he had asked every few hours and the answer was always the same.

"No sir, I don't believe so."

"Can I therefore make a phone call?"

"Sorry sir, that decision's above my pay grade. You will have to wait for Sir Richard." This was always said with a cheeriness that Adrian did not share or return. For two nights now he had been accommodated with blankets and a sheet in something that evidently had once been a cell, and then woken with scrambled egg at the crack of dawn, having spent a largely sleepless night agonising about what to do next. The few people he had encountered in any way had been friendly, not so say cheery.

Both mornings, he had asked when he would be allowed to leave. No coherent answer had ever emerged. Feeling desperate after lunch on the second day, he had ostentatiously packed his rucksack again and walked out of the door – only to be forced back with the kind of camaraderie you might expect of a psychiatric nurse.

"This is insane," he said with feeling. "What is this place?"

That was in fact the main question he had been asking himself. He had been driven out of London, definitely towards Oxfordshire – they had sped along the M40 until the Chilterns, when the car had turned off onto winding back paths and eventually, when he had thoroughly lost his bearings, they had turned into a driveway of an unmarked and innocuous country house with huge box hedges and nobody around.

There was an old chapel and an entrance gate he imagined must be Jacobean and an intricate wood-carved screen inside. There were dull institutional carpets and, as they progressed through the house, the more like a primary school it became, even down to the ancient pegs to hang clothes and the smell of ancient cabbage. Perhaps some school had been evacuated here in the war, he reasoned. Not that this would have explained the cabbage.

There appeared to be nobody around.

Earlier in his career, he had been involved in a Treasury review of the Crown Estates and he had built up a mental picture of most of the government's obscure country houses, owned or leased by the various ministries and departments, but this one – with a hint of Inigo Jones and clearly somewhere in the Thames Valley – rang no bells.

It was here, looked after only by three or four burly men in puffy black anoraks, that he had been incarcerated for the previous two days. As much confused as ever, he had evidently fallen foul of a government department or agency of some kind, but what they were doing about it and who they were, he remained completely in the dark about.

So when they told him Sir Richard would see him now, he received the news with relief but some trepidation. The name had only been mentioned before in relation to the decision about whether he could leave. He had already projected his greatest hopes and fears onto this personage, aware that he was suffering already from some of the peculiar ways that prisoners tend to become dependent on their captors and was determined to be himself and to set out what he wanted. Starting with some answers about Peter.

But instead of being led deeper into the house, he was led out to a waiting blue car, a Range Rover, parked in the extensive drive and obediently allowed himself to be strapped in.

There were signs to Thame in the road a mile or so away and, to Adrian's astonishment, they headed right back onto the motorway.

"Where are we going? Can I ask?"

Silence from the burly driver.

"Is there nothing you can say?"

Still silence. Adrian resigned himself to the road and snoozed fitfully as they hit traffic on the outskirts of London. This was going to be a revealing day, one way or another.

"Come in, come in. You won't mind if I don't get up. It's a bit of a problem with my leg I'm afraid."

There was a strange, musty smell that took Adrian back to what seemed like a bygone age, but he couldn't quite place it, before realising how long it was since he had smelled cigarette smoke in an office. In front of him was a smiling, elderly gentleman in a charcoal grey suit, with half-moon spectacles, peering at him as if he was a housemaster at an ancient public school and Adrian was an erring pupil. The man reached out to an ashtray and inhaled strongly.

"I do apologise, Mr... er, Matinson. Do you?"

Adrian shook his head. He didn't.

He was being offered a cigarette from a box on the desk as he just remembered characters doing on television in the sixties. For a moment, he felt as if he had somehow slipped out of time.

"Now, let's begin. My name is Parsons. Richard

Parsons. I've been hoping to talk to you for some time, so I apologise for keeping you waiting. I hope my people made you as comfortable as they could in the circumstances. Good."

It really was time to say something, and Adrian had been planning a small speech ever since his arrest in Whitehall, but now it seemed somehow to be misplaced. He was being treated with some respect. I must not succumb to flattery and charm, Adrian said to himself, pinching his hand as if he was St Augustine feeling a whiff of lust. I must not be too clubbable.

"Sir Richard, thank you for seeing me," he said. "But I do have to protest that I have been taken in the street from outside my own office. I have been given no explanation whatsoever. I haven't even been allowed to make a phone call, though I'm glad to say that my mobile phone has been returned to me – though I note it has now no charge. I haven't been afforded the most basic rights of anyone who has been arrested, and another thing..."

Sir Richard made great sweeping movements with his hands, and pointed at a lithograph hanging on the wall above his desk.

"Now, now. Mr Matinson. Have you seen this picture? It is of the defence of Lucknow in the Indian Mutiny. Have a look at how staunchly they defend the ramparts. Imagine you were there…"

Adrian felt irritated. "You did hear my complaints, didn't you…?"

"They held the fort until they dropped. It was a critical moment in history and it justified extreme measures. I can't pretend that we're in the same situation now and I can only apologise for keeping you so long – but these are momentous times and, well, we have to be vigilant. Extremely vigilant."

He was very charming and there was an old-fashioned authority about him which Adrian instinctively trusted, though he tried to remind himself how untrustworthy it actually was.

"But then, of course, you have my full apologies. I need to explain a few things to you and I feel sure you will then understand exactly why I have acted as I did – why I needed to be firmer than perhaps is normal these days." He flicked an imaginary piece of cigarette ash off his lapel and smoothed his carefully combed grey hair.

"My feeling," said Adrian, "is that you owe me more than a simple explanation. I think you need to provide me with full transparency about your involvement in the death of Dr Shilling."

Sir Richard gave another flick. "All in good time, I assure you – may I call you Matinson?"

Had he gone back in time? What on earth was the

correct answer to that kind of question?

"Well, never mind. Let's get down to business. You have I believe heard of the Office of the Defender of the Faith."

Adrian's mind reeled. "You mean the ODF?"

"Ah yes," chuckled Sir Richard. "Every inch the modern Treasury mandarin. You prefer acronyms don't you. I assure you that the Office has been in existence for many centuries before anyone began to reduce things to their basic initial letters. In fact it dates back to 1539. Our founder..." He gestured towards a portrait on the wall, which Adrian recognised as a copy of the Holbein drawing of Thomas Cromwell.

"We prefer not to be listed in the Whitehall directories. We keep ourselves to ourselves," said Sir Richard with satisfaction.

"But what is it you actually do?" said Adrian.

"Ah well," said Sir Richard, leaning forward conspiratorially. "We are the arm of government attached to the Royal Household, at least formally, which looks after the monarch's responsibilities as Defender of the Faith. You are familiar with the title?"

Adrian nodded. "But isn't that a little, sort of, archaic?"

Sir Richard gave a laugh of tolerance, the kind of

snigger reserved for women by the captains of all-male golf clubs. "In fact, it is precisely that issue that I need to talk to you about. You have hit the nub of it. Now," – he took a deep inhale. "For nearly five centuries, we have striven, very quietly but I believe very effectively, to make sure that the original faith that King Henry VIII provided for the nation is properly defended. We have managed this for, let us say, many generations and have defended the Protestant faith in these islands..."

Adrian detected a mistier look which rather softened the edges of Sir Richard. "These days, we don't use the old methods. We have close relations with some contacts in Special Branch, and through them we keep tabs on those who want to take us back to the old abuses and corruption. There have been setbacks of course. One of my predecessors allowed Nicholas Wiseman to declare himself Archbishop of Westminster, which was definitely a defeat. The Pope's visit wasn't our finest hour, but generally speaking we have been extremely successful. I regard our work, quiet and efficient, as a good deal more central than the work to root out socialist agitators and religious fanatics. Because – how can I put this most starkly – Protestantism is the central pillar of the British state."

While Adrian was listening to this speech, his mind was reeling. It felt like an extraordinary encounter with the past. He wondered if he was dreaming, as a result of waiting too long in the strange country house. Not only did Sir Richard appear as if he was from another age, but what he was describing was a kind of administrative archaeology. If the story was true, this corner of government was a relic of Henry VIII's machinery for selling off the ecclesiastical social services that existed in a forgotten cleft in the British state. It was like finding a coelacanth, a dinosaur still walking the earth.

Perhaps it had simply been tolerated for generations, by somebody; perhaps it had just been forgotten. But somehow it had survived countless reviews and austerity budgets stretching back over the political landscape of memory. Somehow it had clung on.

"You are wondering, no doubt, like a good Treasury man, how we still manage to pay our way," said Sir Richard, reading his thoughts. "The answer is simple. The wealth of the monasteries was huge. The funds from the dissolution of Glastonbury Abbey were taken by this office as an endowment; they have been invested wisely through the centuries, and they still pay their modest income today. See what I mean? Simple." He smiled proudly as if he had thought of the idea himself.

"But by what right do you still exist?" asked Adrian, feeling nervously infuriated that such administrative anomalies had slipped through successive Treasury nets.

"We prefer to remain in the shadows. We operate quietly. I doubt even if Her Majesty herself has ever heard of us, though of course we continue to serve her interests. And, of course, our legitimacy derives from the crown."

"Does the Chancellor know? Does the Prime Minister know?" asked Adrian.

Sir Richard ignored the question and sat back in his chair, looking Adrian full in the face.

"Now I am about to take you into my confidence. And as a servant of the crown, I must remind you that you are bound by the Official Secrets Act. Everything you hear in this room must remain absolutely confidential."

Adrian realised he was reacting automatically to the admonition to civil servants to do what they were told, and knew he always responded. He knew his limitations. He was no rebel.

"You do understand, don't you, that we will hold you to this secrecy?"

Adrian nodded reluctantly. What else could I do, he said to himself?

"Fine." A piece of paper was thrust in front of him. He signed, and Sir Richard folded it and filed it theatrically. "Now," he said, putting the file in front of him and making sure it was precisely straight, "I'm going to have to tell you a story just to get you up to date."

"I have said already that the return of the Roman Catholic bishops was a serious defeat for us. So was the Oxford Movement, of course. And when the two came together in the controversial shape of Cardinal Manning, my predecessor at the time was extremely concerned. You remember, of course, the role that Manning played in the Great Dock Strike of 1889?"

Adrian searched his memory. "He tried to settle it, didn't he?"

"He interfered," said Sir Richard, with a sour face. "What is more, he cobbled together some jottings by the art critic John Ruskin and gave them to the Pope and we had the Catholic approach to economics, 'Rerum Novarum'. I'm sure you are familiar with Catholic social doctrine and the concept of subsidiarity?"

Adrian was feeling increasingly out of his depth. "You mean the idea that decisions are best taken closest to people."

"Well, something along those lines," Sir Richard smiled tolerantly. "Ironically, it is one of the founding principles of the European Union."

Adrian was now beginning to feel impatient. "But I don't understand what all this has got to do with me."

"Patience, if you please, Mr Matinson. Excuse me a moment." Sir Richard leapt up, with surprising deftness, despite his leg, and slipped out of the room. A moment later, he was back, accompanied by a man in a strange uniform. He looked surprisingly angelic, but well past retirement. Adrian also noticed he was armed with a pistol ostentatiously hanging in a holster. "This is Colonel Sheldrake. He will explain."

Adrian's mind was wandering. He imagined he was walking along the Pilgrim's Way, yew trees and woodlands to the left of him and a gentle slope down into rural England to his right. It gave him a feeling of great power. He stood up and gripped the newcomer's proffered hand rather more tightly than he usually did such things.

It was difficult, now, to wrench himself back from the Old Road, the inexorable pilgrim path, the chalk downs battered by centuries of feet; from the old yew hedges and sacred wells to the Second World War pillboxes – it was hard somehow to hold both experiences in his mind at the same time. It was hard to see what connected them, the rural tradition and the wind and puddles with this rather fetid, forgotten corner of English politics.

"Good to meet you, Matinson," said Sheldrake dramatically, speaking as if he was some bit part player in *The Dam Busters*. "You must understand what has been going on in this country. We have worked extremely hard for many years now to put right one of our most abject failures, which as I'm sure you must realise has been the involvement with the European Union. We have prevented a resurgence of interest in pilgrimages, which has been so regrettable, for example, in Spain, by encouraging the use of the North Downs as a military area – as of course it was. But the EEC and then the EU, that was a setback..."

He looked to Sir Richard, as if for confirmation.

"Yes, go ahead, Sheldrake."

"I don't understand," said Adrian, coming to, out of his semi-hypnotic trance. "What has the European Union got to do with Catholicism?"

Sheldrake looked thoughtful. He must be retired, thought Adrian. They can't possibly have serving officers quite that old, though he was clearly wearing military uniform. Was that badge something to do with the Household Cavalry? Perhaps this was an example of Old Soldiers Never Die. Sheldrake crossed the room and turned back to him.

"Look, Matinson. It has everything to do with it. The European Union was a Christian Democrat, a Roman Catholic project to impose Catholic social doctrine on Europe, and perhaps that was fine for continental Europe. But not for Protestant northern Europe."

"No!" echoed Sir Richard from his desk.

"The EU is a project founded on subsidiarity. It is a denial of a monarch's right to rule. It is precisely this point that the Reformation, in this country at least, was brought about to avert."

Adrian realised his face must have displayed a kind of general confusion. Because Colonel Sheldrake stepped quickly over to a large poster.

"You recognise this?"

"Not specifically, but generally." Was this an art history lesson?

"Indeed. It is a picture of the Virgin Mary from southern Europe, about seventeenth century. Am I right?"

Adrian nodded.

"Right, now, do you recognise these stars around her head? Do you really think it is a coincidence that the European flag includes precisely this same yellow circle of stars?"

For the first time during this strange interview,

Adrian's attention was completely focused. It was true certainly that the European flag was blue with this same circle.

"If you don't mind me saying so, this seems like one of those bizarre conspiracy theories by obscure sects that you find on YouTube."

Sheldrake looked nonplussed. Was it possible he had never heard of YouTube?

It was Adrian's turn to pace around the room. "Look, I'm sorry," he said. "This obviously has some relevance to me, and maybe even my tutor Peter Shilling, but for the life of me I can't see what it is. Maybe you can enlighten me."

The two old gentlemen exchanged glances.

"As you so rightly say, this does concern Dr Shilling," said Sir Richard, taking a deep breath. "You see, Mr Matinson, our understanding was that Dr Shilling had made something of a breakthrough – perhaps historical, perhaps archaeological, which – if it was true – would have great significance for the nation, and in particular for the referendum that is currently being conducted. It is in the interests of the nation that we should not be a member of the European Union. Yes, I know, that is not the view of HM Treasury but it is our view and we, as you might say, take the long view. We try to rise above day to day political necessities."

"If you are actually opposing HM government, I don't see how the Official Secrets Act applies to me."

"Listen carefully, Mr Matinson," said Colonel Sheldrake, a little menacingly. "It is the job of civil servants to serve the government of the day, am I right?"

"Right."

"And one day there is one policy and perhaps the following day there is another one. One department has one policy and another department has something else entirely. And you, as a civil servant, are expected to follow each one to the letter. I am right, as you know. This is very much the same situation. We represent the long-term interests of the monarch, as Defender of the Faith, though the monarch may not be aware of our work on a day to day basis. You are a civil servant. It is your job to help your superiors achieve their objectives. In this situation, if I may say so, we are your superiors."

"You see Matinson," said Sir Richard with a strange smile. "When Dr Shilling made his discovery, he told almost nobody. But we have our sources, and we knew. We have been trying to discuss it with him, and were indeed doing exactly that when he unfortunately collapsed."

"You mean, you scared him to death."

The two men exchanged glances again. Never in

the history of government had two men looked at each other quite so meaningfully.

"I don't think you are in a position to make allegations, Matinson. You would be surprised what kind of powers we have at our disposal..."

Sir Richard interrupted him, holding up a hand with apparently infinite patience. "No, come, come, Mr Matinson. We don't do that kind of skulduggery, I assure you. Not these days."

Adrian's mind was reeling. "So if you have nothing to hide, what do you want of me?"

"The answer is, Mr Matinson, that there is something we don't know and it is absolutely vital for the future of the nation that we do know, and we are asking for your help."

This really was extraordinary. Were these men so unworldly, or so old-fashioned, that they really believed he would help, from some misplaced sense of duty? Did they really believe they had reassured him about Peter's death, accidental or not?

"We believe that Dr Shilling was trying to tell you what he had found, and would have done so if you had met. I believe he had been leaving clues for you along the road that the ignorant know as the Pilgrim's Way. I would like to see those clues, if you would be so good. In fact, I believe, looked at from this point of view, it is your duty to help us."

"I'm sorry, you will have to take me more into your confidence if you want me to help. What did Peter find?"

Sir Richard put down his cigarette and leaned back in his chair.

"I tell you what, Mr Matinson. Let's end this conference now and give you the chance to think about what we have said. I will be calling your superiors at the Treasury to let them know that we have met and then we can talk again early in the morning."

Sheldrake took Adrian gently but firmly by the arm. But Adrian shook him off.

"Hold on, hold on. Please tell me who are the men in the white van who have been following me around? Why was the inquest rushed through? I don't understand what's going on. I don't UNDERSTAND!"

He suddenly felt furious. It must have shown on his face.

"Dear dear, Mr Matinson," said Sir Richard in an apparent imitation of Joyce Grenfell at the nursery school. "I don't think that kind of outburst becomes you. We both want to know things and I'm sure there is some kind of mutually satisfactory arrangement we can make. I will talk to you tomorrow."

"It really is extraordinary that the Remain campaign would have us believe that Britain depends on the Europeans, in some way – that is, the Britain that provided us with Nelson and Wellington and Pitt and gave us a global influence..."

The radio was repeating the endless exchanges that the BBC believed provided some illumination about the issues of the referendum. Adrian sat in the back of the car speeding him back from his encounter with the ODF; they were obviously still chauffeuring him around. He wondered what his superiors at the Treasury would say at the news that this obscure government department had kidnapped one of their senior officials.

He grinned to himself but still felt his mind wandering. He was feeling ridiculously tired and soon found himself musing about whether the Euro referendum campaign marked the end of the peculiar approach which had dominated Treasury decision-making for a decade or so, one that civil servants referred to as 'evidence-based policy'. Really, everything was now disputed – every assertion, every figure, every supposed fact. Nothing was accepted as evidence by the opposing side. There appeared to be no middle ground. The centre could not hold, he said to himself. Now, who wrote that? Was it Yeats? Was it Arnold?

He had not yet decided what he would say to Sir Richard if he was allowed to meet him again as soon as tomorrow, but he worried away at the central problem: what was it that Peter could possibly have discovered that could have bearing at all on the European referendum? It was hard to imagine.

Had he perhaps stumbled on some legal document that regulated our relationship with Europe, or some new claim to sovereignty over France? Why had they mentioned archaeology? Had he dug up something, literally, or were they speaking metaphorically? It had to be metaphorical, hadn't it? In which case, Peter had dug up some set of ideas that must have something to do with the Reformation. Some documented claim by Henry VIII? But what could possibly worry Sir Richard and his gang of Protestant backwoodsmen, that would have any public resonance?

It could only be something involving the original doctrines of the 'Defender of the Faith'. It wasn't Peter's period, but he must have found some inflammatory opinion about the nation's place in Europe. If the clues were leading him to that document, it would at least make some kind of sense.

"The right to rule has been a fundamental principle since the Reformation," someone was saying on the radio. It was Michel Gove introducing a new note, and again Adrian pricked up his ears.

Absolute nonsense, he said to himself. The Reformation idea has been out of date for centuries. It dates back to the day when religious freedom meant the right of a prince to impose whatever religion he wanted on those he ruled. We don't believe in the unfettered rights of princes any more... do we?

The right to rule. Maybe that was what all this was about, thought Adrian. The issue wasn't about democratic control but over the right of the elite to rule unfettered from supranational authority abroad – whether it was from the Pope or the Eurocrats. Brussels and Rome seemed to play parallel roles in the English psyche through history.

Heavens, he told himself, stop, stop. How hard have I tried not to think too deeply and get distracted by the referendum. In any case, I've got work to do. Then the stress and the soporific business of driving down the M40 got the better of him and he dozed, as they sped through the Chilterns and back to that comfortable, gravelly drive.

As they scrunched over it, he woke up and realised he did now know what he was going to do.

The door banged shut and Adrian could hear the

sound of traffic around him and the shouting of tour guides. They were behind Westminster Abbey, walking down ancient, half-forgotten, crumbling stone corridors, past the last banqueting rooms of kings and princes long dead.

His problem, as he knew very well, because he had spent a sleepless night thinking about it, was that his knowledge was extremely partial. He knew more about some aspects of the basic situation than Sir Richard. About other aspects, like the nature of Peter's discovery, he knew less. It was hardly the basis on which to take a decision on how to act. In the background, he kept on wondering what Peter would advise him to do, and also how he might justify whatever he decided later to Barley. Still, he remained reasonably sure he was about to do the right thing. Perhaps even the only thing open to him.

The cloisters were full of memorial stones of eighteenth century gentlemen; as he measured the flagstones dreamily with his feet, he was accompanied by a muscle bound man in an ill-fitting suit who he believed he recognised from the river incident at Snodland. They did not exchange pleasantries.

He fingered the thirty-six hours of bearded growth – he had not been provided with any shaving equipment; he felt it put him at a disadvantage to the suave, and perfectly shaved Sir Richard.

They stooped in the darkness outside what was becoming a familiar wooden door. There was no door sign. It swung open.

"Ah, Mr Matinson. Sir Richard is waiting for you, please go straight in."

Inside, he and Sheldrake were so precisely reprising the positions where he had left them twenty-four hours before, that Adrian wondered for a fleeting moment whether there was some kind of wrinkle in time that allowed these peculiar scions of another age to appear before him – perhaps they only existed when he was talking to them. But he soon dismissed this as tobacco smoke, like an ancient smell strangely evocative of years gone by, wafted towards him.

"Come in, Mr Matinson. Glad to see you again. Do sit down."

Adrian moved towards the black plastic chair, then realised that once again he would be seated too low. He chose instead an upright chair and sat there, daring them to move him.

"So," said Sir Richard. "Have you decided that you will help us?"

Adrian chose his words carefully. He had been choosing them all day.

"The trouble is, Sir Richard, that I know even less

than you do. I have certainly been collecting clues, as your heavies questioned me about earlier. But I have drawn a blank at St Edith's Well, where I found nothing."

There was silence for a moment. "May I see the clues?"

"Unfortunately, I no longer have them."

The two old men conferred quietly together.

"I advise you to co-operate with us, Mr Matinson," said Sheldrake.

"No really, I am happy to co-operate and I can remember the clues and will explain why one led to another. Unfortunately, the trail has now gone cold. When your men caught up with us at Snodland, I was in the process of deciding whether to stop the search."

"Very well then. Tell us."

And Adrian told them the story, right from the moment he had discovered about Peter Shilling's death, and begun his journey along the Pilgrim's Way – the clue in Alresford about the horse thief and in St Catherine's Chapel, and the clue that followed that led him to St Edith's Well. He explained where he had found them but he was careful not to tell them about the package that arrived at his house. Nor did he connect the burglary to them, though the two events were now firmly connected in his own mind. When he reached the well, Sir Richard stubbed out his cigarette.

"I understand from my men that you carried on along the road after that until they caught up with you at Snodland. Why was that?"

"I wanted to continue to the end. As a kind of tribute to Peter... to Peter Shilling. He obviously wanted me to. I would still like to do that."

"If you are not telling me the whole truth..." said Sheldrake, a little menacingly. Adrian ignored him.

"Now, perhaps there is a quid pro quo. I've told you what I know. Perhaps you could reciprocate and tell me a little more about why this is important to you."

Sir Richard and Sheldrake exchanged glances again.

Sir Richard lit another cigarette. "You know what this is all about, don't you, Matinson? It's all about self-determination. It is, has, always has been, about whether we live under the domination of the Papal authority or whether we live under our own. You may think we are a reformed nation, that we have been since Henry VIII, but England actually oscillates between the two, between Catholicism and Protestantism.

The Office of the Defender of the Faith has been watching over the way this happens, and we put out a deft arm, very quietly, every generation or so, to steady the forces of light. Your friend Dr Shilling was definitely on the Catholic side. That was fine. It's a free country, but don't forget *why* it is a free country."

Adrian felt his anger rising. "Actually, he was an Anglican..."

"Yes, but in his attitudes he was an Anglo-Catholic, was he not? He doubted whether Henry VIII was right. He was deeply conservative about the demise of the monasteries. I've read his articles."

Colonel Sheldrake leaned forward. "You must understand; we don't keep people under surveillance or anything, but we keep our ear to the ground and we are alert to anyone bringing back elements of the old faith – anyone who seeks to set up an alternative source of power to the government in London. We have always been vigilant against any attempt to revive the symbols of this kind of opposition. Your friend, Shilling, may have believed himself to be an antiquarian, following abstruse and barely remembered knowledge, but these things have resonance, even now."

"I find it hard to quite share your seriousness," said Adrian.

"Well, you are wrong," said Sir Richard. "Let's set aside all this modern talk about democratic rights of self-determination that they are using in the referendum debate. We all know that is just hocus-pocus to cover up the real issue. *The right to rule ourselves.*"

He reached a kind of crescendo, raising both arms as if he was conducting an orchestra.

Adrian was incredulous. "You seriously mean to tell me that you are concerned to protect the old interpretations – the right of princes to rule, to govern unfettered by supranational authority. That's what all this is about? Really?"

Sir Richard leaned back in his chair. "Of course."

But there was a question that was growing in importance in Adrian's mind and he couldn't stay quiet any more.

"You seem to imply, and I'm sure you'll correct me if I'm wrong, that the Pilgrim's Way is some kind of threat."

"Of course it is," said Sheldrake.

"But nobody even knows about it. Nobody uses it. Nobody has used it at all since Henry VIII took away Becket's shrine and scattered his bones in – when was it?"

Sir Richard interrupted. "In 1538, the year they ended his sainthood. Not before time, either. Mr Matinson, you clearly don't understand the power of these traditions. For three and a half centuries, the Pilgrim's Way was a powerful symbol of resistance to the crown, of moral authority over and above the king. You may say that this is all a very good thing, but it isn't English. It isn't our way. In our country, the English tradition, the British tradition, the king or queen rules without limit."

"But the king hasn't ruled for centuries either. Not unfettered."

"Well, now, of course, the prime minister uses the powers of the monarchs. We don't have any of this nonsense about separation of powers. We get things done in this country."

"I assure you," said Adrian, "we don't get as much done as you clearly think. I work for the outfit."

There was polite laughter. Adrian joined in. These old buffers seemed to him to be deluded remnants of a forgotten age. Almost harmless. But had they not harmed Peter?

"So are you prepared to tell me what Peter Shilling had found and why you are so interested in it?"

Sir Richard stared at him, sphinx-like. "I'm afraid we are not at liberty to say," said Sheldrake. "But we do still require you to be silent on this issue, and there will come a time, probably in the next few days, when we will require your assistance; I am expecting you to be available to help us. And in the meantime, I want you to take us to St Edith's Well and we will have another look. And let me warn you. We have considerable powers to compel your co-operation if you fail us. In fact, let's not beat around the bush: if you fail us or try to pull the wool over our eyes, the consequences for yourself will be extreme."

"Is that what you said to Peter?"

There was a brief silence between them. Then Sir Richard recovered himself.

"The stakes are high, Mr Matinson," he said. "Now I want you to go with our officers and to make a full search of St Edith's Well to see if you've missed something."

X

"It is worth noting, that no part of the Old Road is enclosed for so great a length as that which passes from the western to the eastern lodge of Eastwell Park. Nearly two miles of its course lies here, within the fence of a private owner."

Hilaire Belloc, *The Old Road*, page 264.

As Adrian watched Sir Richard's men searching St Edith's Well, poking, prodding, cracking and shifting the old mixture of concrete and ancient stones, the anger inside him grew like a malignant presence. It wasn't useful to the cause to feel rage. He was unused to feeling anything at all along those lines, certainly about people who were obviously senior civil servants of a kind, and tried hard to suppress it – but he was increasingly unable to.

His anger seemed to burst out of every restraint, every time he tried to shift his mind into another groove, there it was, growing, growing. He tried very hard to adjust his face into the shape of an open-minded, tolerant and effective servant of the people, but was aware that he was failing. Perhaps he was no longer that. Perhaps these last few days had shifted him imperceptibly over the edge to becoming some kind of rebel.

Who did they think they were, these elderly apparatchiks with extra-legal powers? At the very least, they had frightened his old friend to death, and possibly worse. They had taken him virtually prisoner for forty-eight hours and interfered with his line management. They had offered him no real explanation, let alone an apology, yet had left him with a series of vague threats. And now, Colonel Sheldrake was wandering, coolly smoking a cigarette, while his men battered away at St Edith's Well.

It was partly that Adrian was recovering slowly from the shock of his release. Because if he had been unnerved by the tone they used to dismiss him, Adrian had been staggered by the reception awaiting him outside. He had been bundled out of the car and into a military vehicle of some kind, accompanied by six military men in battledress. In their company, he sped, and with a blue light flashing, round the M25 to Kent and on to Kemsing and to the well. They had ignored the handful of traffic lights they passed and piled brashly into the ancient monument, with one man posted at the door and Sheldrake languidly separating himself for a smoke outside.

After half an hour of fruitless searching, and shifting of bricks and breaking of occasional concrete slabs, Sheldrake came in.

"You are sure the previous clue meant this place? Remind me of what the clue said?"

Adrian parroted out the basic words that had led them to St Edith. Sheldrake drew long and deep on his cigarette. "Well, we have three possibilities, do we not? One, somehow, someone got here first, accidentally or on purpose. Two, we have got the wrong place, though that certainly sounds unlikely. Three, you are misleading us in some way. I've given you fair warning about the last of these, so my working hypothesis is probably number one. What do you say to that, Matinson?"

"I think you are quite probably right. There is one more possibility, though: that we are in the right place and we have for some reason failed to find it. Or perhaps Peter just forgot this one. I have no reason to suppose that he was doing anything other than having a joke with me at this stage – before he realised your men were after him."

Sheldrake gave a flash of irritation. "I'll let that pass. Very well." He drew himself up. "Waters. Back to the cars. Now, Matinson, we're going to leave you here. Your rucksack's in the back of the Land Rover and we will be in touch with you in a few days, when you'll be given your instructions."

This was unexpected and not wholly welcome. Adrian had been counting on them to take him back to London.

"But, where can I go? I haven't got much money." He felt it was important to put on a show of reluctance.

"You will find that your credit cards and phone are in the pocket of your rucksack. I bid you goodbye." The soldiers had loaded themselves aboard and they were off. Adrian stared after them, unsure why he had been left to himself. Presumably they were watching him. Probably they were listening to him too; at least he had to assume that. That ruled out calling Barley. No, there was nothing for it. He would have to carry on quietly, by himself and as unobtrusively as possible.

He reached for his mobile phone to see if Sheldrake had really replaced it. There it was, but the battery was dead. He searched through the rest of his belongings and found they had omitted to include his charger.

Adrian had already decided some of what he was going to do. This was clearly a race between himself and Sir Richard whereby both sides were missing crucial facts. He had little idea what Peter Shilling had uncovered which had so unnerved the ODF. Sir Richard and his cronies would not follow the clues because he had destroyed the most recent one. The Euro referendum was now less than a week away and political tension was bound to rise: even without his phone or charger, he was almost certain to hear from them again – though they seemed, on the face of it, to be on the winning side.

The posters were everywhere on both sides, but there was no doubt that the Vote Leave posters were more raucous, more obvious. It looked almost as if Sheldrake and the others were succeeding without his help.

They said with great confidence that they would ask for this help – give him his instructions, for goodness sake – within a few days. It was going to be important to stay off the road as much as possible and to be more than quiet. He had not shaved now for forty-eight hours and, with a bit of luck, he might have something of a beard in a few days' time. He also needed to dye his hair and get a change of clothes. It wouldn't be beyond them to have put some kind of tracer or bug on him somewhere. They may come across as buffoons from the previous century, but they almost certainly derived the benefit of someone's modern IT skills.

The main way forward, as far as he could see, would be to complete the walk along the Pilgrim's Way and find what Peter wanted him to know, and then he would know what to do.

He took a bus to Snodland again, remembering too late that he would need to get over the river. That required some cash, a taxi and a lift to the monastery at Aylesford, where the nearest crossing was. Then it was back on the Old Road, past Boxley, Detling and Lenham and their various pubs.

It was now mid-afternoon and the sun was getting hotter. If he put on a bit of speed, he might make another five or ten miles before dark. He consulted his well-thumbed copy of Hilaire Belloc:

"From Boxley to Charing the Old Road presents little for comment, save that over these thirteen miles it is more direct, more conspicuously marked, and on the whole better preserved than in any other similar stretch of its whole course…"

At Charing, he found a pub and room and was kept awake by the raucous laughter from down below in the bar. Then, in the morning, he woke early, boiled the kettle beside his bed, read the instructions on the hair dye sachet he had bought in Snodland, and set about the great transformation.

By 7am, with wet blonde hair, he was out on the road again, and with renewed enthusiasm. Because, over breakfast of egg and sausage, he had started to think again about the Princes in the Tower, and remembered a story that Peter had told him years ago. It was a theory that neither of the princes had actually been murdered by Richard III – or anyone else – whether or not he had wanted them dead. No, this story was very different. It was suggested that Edward V, the boy king, had died of flu and his younger brother Richard had been released to a very different kind of life. Hadn't he actually become a bricklayer? Wasn't it in Kent somewhere?

He wracked his brain to remember what Peter had said. It was just the kind of abstruse historical wrinkle that Peter had loved – little or no evidence, no serious backing from scholars, but exciting and potentially transformative. Just the kind of thing he had enjoyed, and it would have been like him to have wielded a clue along those lines. If only he could remember.

Adrian stared sadly at his lifeless phone. Nothing. Again, there was no option but to walk on, and it was a beautiful morning. He planned to walk until ten o'clock and then just lie low until the evening. He had no intention of being available or visible enough to be given any instructions by Sir Richard and his gang. Not until he knew more about what Peter had discovered.

Adrian glanced at his watch. It was a few minutes to ten. A beautiful day with a light breeze, far too beautiful a day to waste not walking the Old Road. Yes, Sir Richard's men must have a good idea where he was, but he could see some way ahead on the road, across the fields, where a beech tree wood lay ahead of him and it must be possible to avoid them in there. Then again, he was due back at work the following week...

No, he was going to take the risk of pressing on, and – if he saw suspicious, muscle-bound men waiting ahead of him – he would quietly fade into the landscape. The view was anyway beginning to change. No more long escarpment to his right or lines of yew trees along the way to his left. It was more meandering, more relaxed and more impoverished too: old railway carriages full of Polish hop pickers, their washing hanging from makeshift lines, and tunnels that led nowhere under the railway, and great open fields of abandoned pumpkins from the year before.

Then suddenly, on the edge of another wood, a woman approached him. There had been few enough walkers early in the day – and few enough walkers on the Pilgrim's Way throughout his journey. This woman moved with a familiar gait that Adrian could not place. As she got nearer, she spread her arms out in recognition. It was Barley.

"Good lord, Barley, what are you doing here?" He felt overwhelmingly pleased.

"I'm looking for you, of course. Do you think I make a habit of wandering through woods and fields by myself?"

They hugged, but Barley pulled impatiently away.

"Listen, Adrian, I'm so glad I managed to catch you..."

"What, you mean...?" He felt confused.

"Before you got to the old church of course."

"Sorry, Barley, you'll have to enlighten me."

"Listen, Adrian, get off the path for a moment. We'll go over there, just in case anyone comes by, and I'll tell you."

His mind reeling, Adrian followed Barley into the copse and sat down with her, while she stared watchfully and nervously at the path down which they had just come. There was nobody about. Sheep droppings covered the ground around them. In the distance, was a great ancient manor-house.

"Listen Adrian, just over the brow of the hill, there's an old ruined church. It is called St Mary's, Eastwell. It's mostly overgrown and there's no roof but there's a tomb there..."

Adrian listened with some apprehension, because Barley seemed to be more excitable than usual. He thought of her as languid and calm in the extreme. Now she was animated, as if she had some important news to impart. She spoke far too fast and struggled to catch a breath.

"Slow down, Barley. We've got lots of time."

"Maybe, maybe not. Anyway, I thought of it the day before yesterday. I remembered Peter telling me once, years ago, that you can see the grave of one of the Princes in the Tower. Of course, there's absolutely no evidence for it, and the Richard Plantagenet who was a bricklayer buried in this church might have been somebody else entirely. I suddenly remembered, looked it up, and tried to call you but your phone hasn't been working."

"Well," said Adrian. "Long story. I'll tell you in a moment. They kept my charger. I don't think they meant to. They said they were going to contact me."

"Who did? No, don't tell me. I think I know because I've met them. They've been at the church too. They're over there now. That's why I've met you, to head you off."

Adrian swore and stormed around, perplexed. How could they have known? "I was so careful not to tell them about the most recent clue."

"I think it was my fault. When I thought of it, I left a message on your answerphone. So stupid."

A cold shiver went down Adrian's spine. If they had listened in to his answerphone messages, then they were really determined. They will also have known that he had lied to them.

"Now they've got the clue then, it might even be the last one. We might as well give up. For goodness sake – that's it, isn't it? They've won."

"I don't think so," said Barley. "Not yet." She held out one of the familiar plastic tubes that Peter Shilling had used.

"But how? How did you get it? I don't understand."

She smiled in a mysterious way. "Because I got there first."

XI

"There stood in the Watling Street, that road of a dreadful antiquity, in front of a villa, an omnibus. Upon this we climbed..."
Hilaire Belloc, *The Old Road*, page 277.

Adrian switched on the radio in the Kent guest house where he was staying. Roses wafted towards him from the counterpane. He looked at the digital clock so kindly provided by the establishment. It was five in the morning. Radio 4 was just starting up; he turned it on quietly to cajole Barley into a waking state without the embarrassment and intimacy of actually shaking her awake. The usual headlines, mostly about the referendum: one side had claimed that leaving the EU would torpedo people's pensions. The other side were banging on about controlling borders. "It's all about control," said the Leave spokesman.

He looked at Barley's unwashed face struggling to wake up. Adrian mulled ruefully on the realisation that he had spent another night on opposite sides of the same bed to Barley, but they had both simply fallen asleep within minutes of hitting the mattress. At least, he assumed she had. He certainly had.

The dawn had that cold bleakness about it which made it so hard to wake. He fluttered nervously around her still prone body, lying curled up and breathing deeply.

"Barley?"

A cross between a grunt and a moan emerged.

"It's time to go..."

"Really? Oh God..." She got up in bed, her tousled hair in her eyes, and Adrian realised suddenly, and to his horror, that he loved her as much as ever. He stared at her, drinking her in.

"What are you staring at?" she laughed grumpily. "Haven't you ever seen a woman without make-up before. Honestly," she said, as she skipped lightly to the bathroom. "You bachelors..."

Half an hour later, they had opened their packet of biscuits, put aside their coffees and stepped out into the road. It was a brisk day, and might even promise a little heat. They had six miles to go, and that meant a couple of hours to sort out the meaning of Peter's clues. It was as the dawn seeped into the sky to the east, that Adrian and Barley walked past the huge earthworks where the Romans under Julius Caesar had fought the Celts in a huge pitched battle.

"Impressive isn't it," said Adrian.

"Yes, and a bit unexpected. When was it? The battle, I mean? I can't believe I'm forgetting all this old stuff that Peter taught me. Was it 55 BC?"

"I think it was 54."

Barley nodded her head in recognition. "Oh well, I'd really like to go up there and watch the dawn."

"We haven't got time," said Adrian, feeling like a spoilsport. "Not if we want to get to Canterbury sometime today."

"Still, let's pop up there for a moment, shall we? Pop up for a peer..." She laughed and, without waiting for an answer, plunged up the hill.

For the last few hours, the two of them had been walking hard through woods and housing estates, from their night in the picturesque village of Chilham. It was clear that, if it hadn't been for Belloc's journey in early years of the previous century, there would be little or no memory of the Old Road for great stretches of it as it headed on the last few miles into Canterbury.

They had decided to walk from the early hours of the morning, aware that Sir Richard's men of the ODF would probably be less likely to watch the route then, and to sleep during the main hours of daylight.

It was unseasonably hot as well, which also gave the arrangement other attractions. Barley still had a day to go before she had to return home to take over management of her children and to dispatch them on her ex-husband's yacht trip across the Channel.

"You know, Barley," said Adrian, as they reached the top and gazed out just above the level of the trees in the surrounding woods. "I really like walking with you. It's beyond the call of duty to come with me like this."

She looked at him coyly.

"Oh, it's the same as you really. I want to finish the Pilgrim's Way because that's what Peter wanted. I'm doing it as a small thank you to him."

A little chastened by this reply, Adrian ran the last few steps to the very top of Bigbury Camp and looked over to where the dawn was now complete, and there it was – the tower of Canterbury Cathedral – rising against the morning. There was no echoing sound of medieval choirs or plainsong, as there would have been if this had been a film. Just an expectant silence.

"That's where we're heading," he said.

"Right," she said, and took his hand.

Adrian squeezed hers, acutely aware that they were falling back into their original pattern: the shared room in the guest house in Chilham the night before, where they had both stayed resolutely on their own side of the large double bed, was all too familiar. The truth was that there had not been the sign of any kind of desire or encouragement from Barley. It was almost as if she was unaware that, somewhere deep inside this Treasury mandarin, was a sexual being.

"You know, Barley. When you got cross with me in the car going to London..."

"Oh that – I'm so sorry Adrian. I shouldn't have lost my temper..."

Yes, yes, thought Adrian, walking a little faster. The sticks and twigs cracked below his feet as he went.

"But what did you mean? Did you mean that there is..." – he was aware he was choosing his words badly. For goodness sake don't let's be self-deprecating. "Did you mean we might have a second chance?"

"Or a third or fourth chance?"

"Hold on! What do you mean?"

Her face clouded for a moment as they swung along the route the old pilgrims had taken.

"I don't know, Adrian – what do *you* mean? You never really wanted me all those years ago, I know you pretended to. Maybe you even pretended to yourself, but..."

Adrian was suddenly cross. "You can't possibly think that I was somehow..." Then he stopped short. Had he been so obscure? Had he really never made himself clear? He sighed powerfully. "Look, never mind now. We've got other things to think about. Get that clue out again."

The sun was up now and there was a heavy, potent mist across the fields in the distance. They were crossing a huge fruit farm with the basic huts and washing of maybe hundreds of immigrant pickers trapped in a basic life of apples.

Barley reached inside her voluminous pockets and pulled out the crumpled piece of paper. Adrian looked at it. The clue said:

"My first clue and now your last.
The saint is gone, and those days are past.
The saint is sleeping but you can wake
him, if you can knit them for his sake:
Put these clues together, and in thrall;
link them up and you'll know all."

"Well, I'm guessing the saint in question is St Thomas Becket, since we are now in the vicinity of Canterbury," said Adrian. Barley took no notice.

"It seems to be telling us to put the clues together," she said, staring at the filthy piece of paper. "But we've had this conversation already a couple of times."

They had indeed, going round and round. How were they to link the clues together? Did the lines spell out something like an acrostic? Were they supposed to mix and match in some way? But they had tried and failed.

"The question is," said Barley, "what does he mean: 'put these clues together'?"

"It's time we had a break, isn't it."

The sun was now high in the sky. If the ODF wanted them, they would know where they were likely to be, so once the morning was well and truly upon them, it would have to be time to get off the Old Road and get a taxi back to Barley's car. There were still two miles to go to get to the cathedral.

Barley stood still for a moment and put out her arm, as if she wanted to arrest him.

"Look Adrian, I've got to get home by tomorrow, because I'm meeting the kids and taking them down to Rob's yacht in Chichester Marina. I know, he's only just had them, but well – that's what we've agreed. Anyway, I don't want to leave quite yet. But if we can get to the cathedral, I'll at least feel I've achieved something for Peter, even if I haven't exactly cracked his code."

Adrian examined her face to see what secret messages were there. He was as flummoxed by her expression as they were about Peter's code.

"Would you come all the way with me then?" he hesitated, aware of his *double entendre*. "I mean come to the end?"

"I'm not sure it's going to be the end, exactly. But when we've cracked the code, I want to know why your previous marriage didn't last..."

"The way I see it is this," said Barley as they reached the outskirts of Canterbury. "Somehow we have to put together all the names in some kind of order. Each of the clues is about names, right? – John Hammond, and now Thomas Becket."

A list of names? Now they were getting somewhere. Adrian stepped forward with renewed energy, his mind reeling as much as it was possible to reel after someone had been awake since five. "Is it some kind of anagram with their names? Hey," he said, suddenly wondering. "Do you think there's another clue in the cathedral?"

"Well, he did say this one was our last, didn't he?"

Fair enough. She was right, but don't let's lose the energy. "OK, let's try it and spell it out – starting with the H for Hammond.

"Does that spell anything? We don't have a surname for St Edith. Or St Catherine come to that..."

"OK, let's just do first names: J and W, then C and E. Then R and T. Not enough vowels. It can't be that."

They were walking through a waking suburb now. There were street lamps, though the sun was now high in the sky, greeting the morning. People were getting into their cars for their morning commute. Men in dark waist-length anoraks were zipping themselves up to travel all the way to some building site or other. Mothers were putting their children into care for the day. Cleaning contractors and their bleary-eyed cleaning staff were making their way towards their morning bus stops.

"Are they the initials for something? No, that's too ambiguous."

"Unless they're numbers? Hold on, Adrian. I think that's it. It's very simple, actually. It's a number, a map reference perhaps? Or a membership number – no, I bet you it's a *phone* number."

Adrian was getting irritated.

"How can it be a number? Oh, you mean corresponding to their position in the alphabet." He began counting the alphabet on his fingers. "That's

10, 23, 3, um... 5, 18 and 20.

"Doesn't really solve it, does it. Let's write it down..."

They searched their pockets and Adrian found an old train timetable. They wrote it down and puzzled over it. Time passed. Two buses went by.

"We can't stop here staring at numbers for ever. What does the clue mean about adding the zero?"

"Yes," said Barley, close to giving up again. "It's typical of Peter to do something like add a random zero. How can any self-respecting cryptographer understand that sort of stuff?"

There were the gates of the old city ahead of them. It looked dark and sinister in the morning light, out of place somehow amidst the traffic. But it gave them a spring in their step, and pumped more energy into their aching legs. They were nearly there, and maybe heading towards some kind of resolution. "I'd be hard-pressed to say what I was hoping about this place," said Adrian. "Hold on, that's funny..."

They had walked past the sharp turning to St Dunstan-Without-the-Westgate and crossed the Stour, when the bells from the cathedral began to ring out.

"It isn't Sunday."

"How English you are," said Barley, without looking at him. "As if bells could only be rung on Sundays..."

They walked a little further, too tired really to converse. "Perhaps the cathedral is calling us," she said. "Perhaps it's Peter."

"Or St Peter. Isn't that who the cathedral's dedicated to?"

"No, I think it's Christ himself."

Adrian laughed. "Honestly, who would go walking with a history graduate? I expect my companions to be amazed at my erudition."

"Actually, I think it might be both of them..."

"Stop it! Stop it!"

This time, they both laughed. They were walking down the cobbled streets that once echoed to the sound of the pilgrims, looking upwards towards the ancient tower, as they came closer to the cathedral. It was only when they came to the great gates of the Cathedral Close that they stopped dead.

"Wait!" said Adrian, grabbing Barley's arm. "It's full of soldiers."

They stayed still, then drew back into the shadows.

"Can I help you, miss?" said a man in military uniform.

"Oh no, just looking thanks," said Barley with a

little laugh. He regarded them suspiciously for a moment and then looked down.

"Hey, I think you've dropped your phone number. Is it for me?" He leered at Barley. She brushed the fringe out of her eyes and accepted the scrap of paper. It had fallen out of her pocket.

"Thank you so much. I didn't want to lose that!" she said, lightly. She glanced at the scrap. "In any case, it isn't my phone number." She nodded towards Adrian. "It's his!"

The soldier moved off, still chortling idiotically.

"What are they looking for? Judging by the expression on their faces, I'm not sure they know either. But I suppose it could possibly be us."

"Shall we turn around, just in case?" said Barley sadly.

"How can we, when we've come so far? In any case, it can't really be us, can it?"

Adrian reached into his rucksack and drew out Hilaire Belloc's book.

"As I had so fixed the date of this journey, the hour and the day were the day and hour of the murder," he read...

"The weather was the weather of the same day seven hundred and twenty-nine years before: a clear cold air, a clean sky, and a little wind. I went into the church and stood at the edge of the north transept, where the archbishop fell, and where a few Norman stones lend a material basis for the resurrection of the past. It was almost dark.... I had hoped in such an exact coincidence to see the gigantic figure, huge in its winter swaddling, watching the door from the cloister, watching it unbarred at his command. I had thought to discover the hard large face in profile, still caught by the last light from the round southern windows and gazing fixedly; the choir beyond at their alternate nasal chaunt; the clamour; the battering of oak; the jangle of arms, and of scabbards trailing, as the troops broke in; the footfalls of the monks that fled, the sharp insults, the blows and Gilbert groaning, wounded, and à Becket dead. I listened for Mauclerc's mad boast of violence, scattering the brains on the pavement and swearing that the dead could never rise; then for the rush and flight from the profanation of a temple, and for distant voices crying outside in the streets of the city, under the sunset, 'The King's Men! The King's!'..."

"No, you're right," said Barley when he had finished reading. "Let's go in. If something happens and we get separated, I'll call you when you're back home."

Adrian thought quickly. That wouldn't work; ODF would hear any phone calls they made to each other. They needed a code – two rings would mean one arrangement, four rings another, then he would put down the receiver.

"No, we've got to separate. I'll meet you here in one hour. If I don't come, call my friend Nadia at the Treasury and tell her everything, she's the only one I can trust. Then, if I get out again and we miss each other, I'll call you at home and ring off. Is that OK? Then I'll call you from a public callbox, at your neighbours'? Does that make sense?"

"OK. I'm taking the children down tomorrow afternoon to their father's yacht, for goodness sake. They're quite old enough to go by themselves really..."

"So have we agreed? Two rings and I'll call you at the number you gave me of your next door neighbours."

"Got it. Good plan."

Then a strange faraway look came into her eyes.

"Adrian, I've just realised something. Don't go yet." She rootled in her pocket and pulled out the crumpled piece of paper again.

"This is the piece of paper we wrote down the numbers on. The soldier must have picked it up upside down. You realise these numbers mean nothing left to right, but right to left, they could just be a phone number. They could be. But only if you *add a zero*."

Adrian's spirits soared again.

"You mean 02 then add the zero? 08, then... You could be right, Barley. We can't use our mobiles to try it in case they are monitoring."

"No, but I can do it, I saw a phone box back there. I'll follow you in. See you in a moment."

Adrian watched her back view disappearing into the crowd, determined and erect. She fascinated him again. He knew she did. It all seemed like another disturbing revelation, given him by Peter, somehow. If only...

Adrian plunged into the gloom through the side door to the left of the West Front. Inside, there were even more soldiers than outside. They milled about with a directed enthusiasm. There seemed to be some kind of altercation between a small group of them and a priest who was denying them entry to the choir stalls. A man with the military bearing of a peculiarly immaculate uniform was striding towards them.

As Adrian walked quietly up the North Transept, he could hear their voices raised.

"Listen, I don't know whose permission you have

to be here and I don't really care. You can't have soldiers all over the cathedral. I don't care *who* you're searching for..."

"OK, Mason, you can leave this to me." The officer had arrived at the melee. His voice sounded familiar. "Let me show you my pass. I am here on the authority of the Queen."

Adrian started as he recognised Colonel Sheldrake. He wasn't looking friendly.

The priest was having none of that. "Yes," he said. "Well, I'm here on the authority of God and I'm telling you – no, I'm *instructing* you to get your men out of my cathedral unless they are actually praying."

Could he slip away without being noticed? Were they really looking for him or was he some kind of cog in a much greater story, some tacked on extra paragraph which he didn't really understand himself.

It was then that a shout from behind told him it was too late.

"Stop! Sir, I think that's him."

Adrian abandoned his rucksack and made for the eastern end of the cathedral. As he reached the chancel steps, they were on him. One soldier grabbed his legs and another pinioned his arms in a half-nelson. He could hear the sound of grinding chairs and shouts and pandemonium as the officers began to exert some kind of order. Beside him, two priests were also being held down. Perhaps they had complained too loudly. Then Sheldrake was next to him.

"Mr Matinson. I said we would be in contact, and now we are. Though you are not the main reason we are in the cathedral today, it is nonetheless useful to have more than an eye on you. I warned you against lying to me and you still lied. I wasted a morning at St Edith's Well, which I'm unlikely to get back."

Adrian tried to reply but had no breath. His head was being held close to the floor.

"Now, do you see this pass?" Sheldrake was waving something in his direction. "It gives me the authority to roam the Queen's estates – and we are in one of her churches – and to make what arrests I may. No, I'm not arresting you, I hasten to add, but I am encouraging you into my custody. Let's put it like that. Just until the big vote is safely over next week."

"Colonel, will you please order your men to act with more restraint in the cathedral? And when you've done that, can you please leave." The troublesome priest was back.

"My dear padre..."

"Please don't call me that."

"Please don't misunderstand me. I have full authority to be here with my men and it's for the good of this cathedral that I'm doing the Queen's work. If you interfere with that, I will arrest you. Now, please will you conduct us outside and I will disturb you no longer. My men, however, will stay here."

"If you insist. And if you must arrest people, please refrain from doing so here. You must realise you're on the very spot where Becket was murdered."

Adrian chuckled to himself. Of course, they were on the chancel steps. It was here where four soldiers sent by Henry II had killed Becket in 1170. He was in august company. But he also had somehow to slip away, if he possibly could.

Sheldrake looked down at him with distaste. "Take him out to my van," he said to the soldiers. Two of them gripped Adrian tightly and took him firmly, but forcibly, back down the nave and out of the cathedral. The other soldiers were looking sheepish now, as if they had been caught napping. Cathedral visitors, those who could see what was happening, stared awkwardly and in a disconnected English way, as if they were wondering whether this display had been organised for their benefit. Adrian could see intense conversations and gesticulating among the cathedral staff.

His mind was working fast. He still had no idea what they were so scared of, or even if it was really his own presence there that worried Sheldrake and his superiors. He realised his heart was racing. Was he due for some kind of punishment? Would they finish him off as they had done to Peter?

He had not thought seriously of escape until he found himself amidst a large group of visitors outside in the close, apparently from the Mothers' Union, under a large banner. They were very obviously praying. The soldiers stopped, unsure whether they should continue across this fervent circle. They began to be jostled a little in the crowd. Adrian felt their grip on him relax as they looked nervously around for a way through. One of them let go to clear a path. Adrian took a deep breath and leaned over to the left, bringing his elbow up and violently down into the man's solar plexus. He doubled up and let go. Suddenly there was pandemonium.

The other gaoler shouted. The Mothers' Union representatives turned on him, and by then Adrian had bolted into the crowd, dodging around to the left. He soon found himself running alongside some ruined walls, unsure where to go. Behind him, he could hear the raucous shouting of the soldiers. He found himself in the cloisters, wondering how he could change his appearance quickly. He slowed his pace so as not to attract attention, though he was now breathing heavily. He was aware that faces were turned towards him, afraid that he was having an asthma attack. He wondered whether he was in fact doing so.

He pulled back a large black curtain on an impulse, as he passed, opened the ancient wooden door he found behind and found himself once more in the quiet of the cathedral. He pulled the door to after him. He turned round and was suddenly face to face with the priest who had been remonstrating with Sheldrake.

They stared at each other for a moment as they realised when they had last seen each other, only about ten minutes before.

"Quick," said the priest, making a sudden decision. "Come with me."

There was no time to decide if this was a good idea or not. Adrian followed. The man took him through a small door in the side of the crypt and down some worn steps into a corner of the undercroft.

"I don't know who you are, but there is something going on here that I don't like," said the priest. He turned to Adrian suddenly. "Give me your word. Let me look at you while you tell me now, truthfully, that you're not a terrorist."

"Not only am I not a terrorist, but I'm on the staff of the Treasury," said Adrian, aware that he was sounding pathetic, and looking nervously behind him.

"Then I'm going to help." He looked deeply into Adrian's eyes a moment longer, as if trying to discern some confirmation of his story. "Come here. You're about my height. He opened a cupboard and pulled down a long black cassock. "I suggest you put this on and come with me."

It only took a moment or two for Adrian to don the black robes. "Ready? Right, now follow me and do exactly as I do."

There was another door, and it looked dark and musty beyond it. "Keep your eyes down here. You may find this a little disturbing."

"Why?" said Adrian, then he saw the lines of dusty, broken, crumbling coffins of the long dead, stretching far into the murky distance.

"Don't worry, it's only a few yards, and they can't hurt you like the living can."

Then they were through and coming along a passage that seemed to slope upwards, then through another wooden door, and up some stairs, past brooms in a cupboard, until they found themselves suddenly in the cafe. The retired couples eating their lunch barely looked up to do more than glance at two vergers emerging from the cupboard and stepping across their vista.

As they crossed the lawn, Adrian could see a number of soldiers drawn up in the distance and looking the other way. Others were in small teams and were beginning to search the ruins he had passed just after he had given his gaolers the slip.

Adrian's mind was racing. He no longer had his rucksack. Or his phone or his change of clothes, or anything very much except what he carried in his memory. He had a little money in his back pocket, but where could he go? Barley would hardly welcome him turning up, with her children in Farnham.

His priest friend was tapping him on the shoulder. They had reached a small lychgate and he was gesticulating in that direction.

Adrian shook his hand. "Thank you. I owe you."

"Oh, I'm just trying to do my best," said the priest apologetically. "Very Anglican..."

Adrian shook his hand and walked quickly out into the street, as he passed the two soldiers on duty, who gave him barely a look. He realised his cassock was just long enough to cover his muddy boots.

In five minutes' brisk walk, he found himself back in the street. There were crowds gathering, some of them campaigning on both sides in the referendum, some of them just aware that something was going on at the cathedral and who wanted to see what it was. He felt anonymous and his heart leapt at the opportunity to escape again. Just as he was wondering how to get in touch with Barley he glimpsed her inside a cafe, eating a large ham sandwich.

She did a double take through the window when she realised who he was.

"Adrian! My God, what's happened to you? I thought I saw you being carted off by the soldiers," she whispered a few moments later.

"We can't stay here. Look, I'm going back to London. I don't think we should go together. I'm going to the station. Can you possibly lend me twenty quid for the train? No, make that thirty. I've got the rest."

"Listen Adrian," she said, reaching into her purse. "I tried the number on the phone. I'm not going to say what we did in case there's someone listening again, but I did what we discussed and it works. You can remember the numbers, can't you? You try, then, as soon as you get back to London. Use a payphone just in case. Good luck, Adrian..." She stood up and waved him out of the shop, still in his cassock.

Now, why didn't I kiss her goodbye, he said to himself?

Of all the things that Adrian found himself worrying about as he walked as fast as he could towards Canterbury railway station, he knew something else was bugging him in the background. He realised soon enough that Barley's farewell had disappointed him. It hadn't somehow been fulsome enough, not passionate enough. It had been too detached. As if she hadn't cared enough. She must have been tired, after all.

It bothered him so much that he barely had time to consider that the railway station would be watched as well. Instead of walking in, he grabbed a taxi outside and asked to be driven to Canterbury East instead. It was worth spending £10 on the precaution. If only he still had his debit cards but, even if he had, he would simply give away his whereabouts if he used them. He would have to call later to get them cancelled.

There were sirens in the distance as he drove away, hoping they weren't for him.

Ten minutes later, the station hove into view. He bought a ticket to Faversham – it was as much as he could afford – and planned to blag his way to solve the problem of the barriers when he reached London.

The journey gave him a little time to think. All he needed was enough money to make a phone call, from a call box if such things still existed. He realised he looked a mess, like some crazy clergyman. But it was worth a try.

At Victoria Station, he got out. He had removed the cassock and found an old carrier bag to stash it. He planned to tell the ticket inspector at the gates that he had overslept and needed to get some money out of the bank, and if necessary leave his name and address. In the event, the gates were open anyway, and he walked purposely along Victoria Street, turned left at Parliament Square with Big Ben towering over him and strode with increasing confidence towards his office in Horse Guards Parade.

"I'm here to see Nadia," he said to the security man on the front door, a little more informally than he had intended.

"Up the stairs and to the left."

Instead, Adrian walked straight on and was lucky enough to find a security guard he knew inside. "I've been called back to the office," he said. "Was on holiday, haven't shaved. No pass. Can you possibly let me through?"

"Oh, go on then, Mr Matinson." He was in, then up in the lift and a few minutes later he was at his desk.

"Hi, yes, I know," he said to the raised faces near

where he sat, in one of the offices off the main corridor. "I'm just popping back for some papers and to make a quick phone call... Yes, really good holiday, in fact, thanks. I've managed to miss all the fuss about the referendum."

"Yes, dammit, you dropped us in it, didn't you!"

By the time they had finished joshing him, he had reached the phone. He pulled out the copy of the Metro newspaper, on which he had noted the numbers from Peter's clues and turned them upside down: they now read like a London number.

He had made a note of the number that Barley had called on the train home, having checked and double-checked the code. The first names of all the people who Peter Shilling had referred to had turned into a London phone number. But in his typical slapdash way, Peter had somehow provided them with a system that only worked if you added a zero for the 020.

He had to assume that not even the ODF would have bugged the Treasury. With excited fingers, he dialled the number. It answered almost immediately.

"The Vault storage repository. For reception, please press 1; if you are an existing customer please press 2; if you want to use our services for the first time, please press 3. For any other matter, please press 0."

He pressed zero.

"Hello. I may have a wrong number. Could you possibly help me?"

"This is the Vault. Is that what you need?"

"Could you give me your address?"

"Postal address? Yes, it's 267 London Road, London SW18 6GH."

"And your nearest station?"

"Wimbledon Common." That made sense. Near Peter's flat.

"Thank you very much. I'll be there tomorrow, if that's OK."

"Fine. We open at nine."

Then suddenly he remembered. Of course. The key that had arrived in the post. Thank goodness that, in all the melodrama of the first day of these peculiar events, he had had the foresight to stick it under the lining of the pond in his back garden at home. It could even still be there.

XII

"It was an upheaval like that by which, in the beginnings of terrestrial life, the huge and dull sea-monsters first took to the keen air of the land. Everything was in the turmoil which the few historians who have seen the vision of this thing have called, some an anarchy, and others a brief interlude of liberty in the politics of Europe. It was neither one nor the other:
it was the travail of a birth.
Hilaire Belloc, *The Old Road*, page 83.

"I'm Adrian Matinson. I called earlier."

He had arrived at the address he was given to find that this was indeed a furniture deposit, and he was told as much again by the very attractive girl on the reception desk.

"Oh yes, of course, Mr Matinson. You have your key? Right – it's a box number..." She looked at the key that Adrian held in his hand. "That's it, box number 936. That's on the second floor. Do you want me to show you up?"

"No, thank you. I'll be fine," said Adrian, deliberately cutting down conversation to a minimum. He found he was shaking with... what? Nerves? Anticipation? Fear? Perhaps a bit of all three, he told himself as he climbed to the second floor.

In fact, Adrian was beginning to feel a little less fearful. He had gone home and crept into his own house for the first time in nearly a fortnight, through the back garden, via a hole in the fence that he had been meaning to mend for nearly a year. He went straight to the front window, noticing that there was still dried blood at the foot of the stairs from when he had been hit over the head. He looked carefully up and down the street until he had convinced himself his house was no longer being watched. He could not be too careful.

The house itself was a terrible mess. As he suspected, every inch had been investigated by someone. Books lay in piles, papers had been taken out of files. Clothes had been strewn around. He feared the hiding place he had used had been found, but managed to prevent himself from creeping out into the garden until after dark. There he lifted two large rocks from beside the pond and was able to pull up the pond lining enough to slip his hand underneath. The envelope had almost disintegrated in the damp but its contents were still there. There was the key. He examined it. It had a number attached to it on a metal label. It was marked 936.

He had crept out again that night, phoned the number and left a message to make an appointment for the following morning.

The carpet inside the repository was made up of those fake rubber squares, with flicks of grey in them. His heart was thumping as he made his way across the squares and up the stairs.

What would he find in the room? Would the key even work?

He was alone in the corridor. There was the number 936. He fiddled with the key, turned it the other way up and – after a heart-stopping moment of doubt – the door opened.

The room was large with a small window so that, at first, he could see nothing. Then he realised that, in the corner, there was a blue hold-all. He went over and knelt in front of it, his hands shaking. He unzipped the bag.

Inside was something the size of an oversized shoebox, wrapped in old newspapers, dating – he checked the dates – back to 1991. It was evidently French. There were news stories about the Gulf War and President Chirac. He unwrapped one layer, then another, until all that covered what seemed like a heavy metal box was a piece of stained and ancient muslin cloth. Inside that was a lead casket, grizzled and black with age. It seemed to be sealed shut, whether locked or simply encrusted with age, he could not tell.

He looked back inside the bag. There was an envelope. He opened it – it had already been read – and there was a letter written and addressed to Dr Peter Shilling, without an address. One glance at it and Adrian changed his mind. He put the letter in his pocket and zipped up the bag again with the metal box. He lifted them up onto his shoulder. It was surprisingly heavy. Then he locked the door behind him and headed back downstairs.

"Thank you for all your help!" he shouted behind him.

Outside in the street, he found himself by a south London station he had never heard of with a taxi company next door. He ordered a cab. "Can you take me to Westminster?" he said.

It wasn't until he was safely inside the car and travelling in light traffic towards Parliament Square that he dared open the envelope again.

Dear Dr Shilling,

You will find inside this bag the item we discussed. I am grateful to you for agreeing to take it into your possession for the time being, pending some kind of safer solution. You will understand from what I say here why I am anxious about providing you with a new address. I don't really want to be contactable. But I am also anxious, after all I've been through – and after all the efforts of generations of my ancestors – that the contents should remain safe.

I promised that, in return, I would write you a full account of my experience since inheriting the item. I believe this will also serve to protect me, because I am depositing a copy with my solicitors in Maidenhead with instructions that they are to make this document public if anything should happen to me, which at times I have felt was likely to be sooner rather than later.

Let me first explain something as I have come to understand it, of how my family came to be involved at all. My ancestor was the son of a canon of Canterbury Cathedral in the 1530s. I know that sounds scandalous, but it did happen in those days, and not just among the Protestants who wanted to have married clergy. Apart from being a member of the de Stone family, I honestly knew nothing about any of this until about five months ago when I received this letter out of the blue from a French attorney in Toulouse.

I did know my great aunt, Cecile de Stone, and even knew she had died, though I'm not aware of having met her since we encountered each other at some kind of house party around 1958. I know that because it was around the time of my twenty-first birthday and I remember how kind she was about meeting an unknown – to her at least – great nephew. I was even aware that there was some family secret that stretched way back, but I had no inkling about what it might be and, to be frank, not a great deal of interest.

I was retired and my time was largely my own and so, when the letter told me that my aunt had left me some money and what they described as "an item of great value" – I think that's how it was expressed – I thought, why not pop down now on a cheap flight and see the French solicitor for myself? I thought it might be fun. I even thought the trip might pay for itself, though I suppose an inheritance is an inheritance and it would have made its way to me one way or another.

I was a librarian before I took early retirement from Croydon Borough Council so I'm not that well off, and small legacies are important for me. I don't get them very often.

It was a peculiar journey, because I was pestered by two rather dubious and unsavoury characters on the way and even on the plane, which I thought nothing about at the time. It was only when I reached the attorney's office that I began to wonder a little at what I had been let in for.

It was the most extraordinary office, like you imagine a lawyer's office might have looked in Dickens' day, perhaps the one in *Great Expectations*. It was full of papers piled high and I swear I even saw a candle and a quill pen. I was led in to meet the man who was described in English as my family solicitor; my aunt had lived in France for many years, and so had her parents and their parents before them – though they maintained establishments in England too – and I believe she went to live there herself when she inherited a considerable sum from another de Stone relative a long time before I was born.

"My English is not perfect, I fear, Monsieur," he said as he motioned me to the chair. The whole impression was somewhat gothic and he took a moment to order another log of wood placed on the fire. M. Leclerc was elderly, fastidious and carried a small *pince-nez*, as if he had been born in an earlier century – as maybe he had, as far as I know.

I said I really didn't mind. My French is a little rusty, I'm afraid.

"You realise, Monsieur, that you have been left a considerable legacy, about 200,000 euros, but there are rather strict conditions attached to the will of your aunt."

"Oh yes?" I said, I see now, rather innocently.

"Oui, Monsieur. It concerns a very ancient artefact that I am now at liberty to disclose to you, but which – when I have told you – you and I will be the only people in the world to know about. But I have to ask your word, in memory of your aunt – my condolences by the way – that you must also tell no one. No one, you understand? *Il est de la plus haute importance.*"

I nodded of course. Who would not have done? But I must say I was pretty dumbfounded already and was even more so when he solemnly got up, shut the door and locked it.

"*Alors.* Now, I may speak freely. You may not know this, but your ancestor, Father William de Stone, was a prominent canon at Canterbury Cathedral at the time of the English reformation. In fact, he was there, *mon ami*, at the moment when King Henry VIII's commissioners were arriving to dissolve the monastic order. It was up to him to rescue as much as he could of the remains of St Thomas Becket before they were destroyed on orders of the king – as the remains of anyone who was revered for standing up against a king could hardly expect to survive. Very bravely, Father de Stone took Becket's head in a leaden box and smuggled it, I believe in a laundry basket, to be delivered to a trusted family outside. From there he rescued it some days later and took it to France where he had relatives.

"You don't mean to say that Aunt Cecile...?"

"I do, *mon ami*. That is exactly what I mean to say. The head of your Thomas Becket was left in the safekeeping of your family four, no nearly five, centuries ago, and it has been passed on from father to son and occasionally to nephew or niece or daughter, with a sum of money that was invested wisely at the time of the dissolution, and has paid over the years to secure the object from unwanted intrusions."

"Are you saying that Aunt Cecile has left it to me? For safekeeping?"

"Actually, it is more complicated than that. Miss de Stone wants the arrangement to end with you, and the condition of the will is that you take charge of this item and make sure it goes back to England and is secured there, in the safekeeping of antiquarians and where it can be revered."

"She wants me to take it home?"

"If you are prepared to accept this task."

"And if I am not?"

"Well then, regretfully Monsieur, I cannot allow you to inherit the money, because it will be left elsewhere."

Well, as you can imagine perhaps, Dr Shilling, I thought this was a relatively simple task. I knew people at the National Trust and one or two other places and I didn't think this job, which I accept was sacred in a way, was too difficult. I said yes, signed the papers and then, from under his desk, M. Leclerc brought out the leaden casket that you see before you now.

It is surprisingly heavy, as you can see and the age of it alone makes it a most extraordinary relic. For a moment, I could think of nothing to say, but I thanked him, agreed on arrangements about the money in the fullness of time and I bid him farewell.

On his advice, I did not board the plane again, but hired a car and drove to Calais and paid enough to drive it all the way home to Sussex, where I live now. My wife died some years ago, so there was really nobody to tell. If I had taken his advice and kept my mouth firmly shut, I am convinced that would have been that. The mistake I made, I believe, was to take the casket to an expert at the Victoria and Albert Museum.

I didn't know them and I think maybe that was how the news leaked out, though I certainly told them almost nothing about what was inside the casket. Nor did they open it, but they were fascinated of course and I have a feeling they guessed something of the kind. It was obvious it was designed as some kind of reliquary. I understood from M. Leclerc that Becket's remains have been missing for centuries.

So two days after the visit to the museum, back again in Sussex, I had a rather unwelcome visit from a man who described himself as Sir Richard Parsons, and who was extremely smooth but rather alarming. He asked to see the casket and I said I had taken the precaution of placing it somewhere safe outside London. In fact, as you know, I had lodged it at the flat of a friend, without telling him what it was.

When I told Sir Richard he could not see it, he became rather unpleasant and threatened me with the Official Secrets Act, though I couldn't see how I had given away any official secrets – quite the opposite in fact. His next threat, that I would be charged with exporting valuable artefacts of national value – or some such – worried me considerably more. Or was it *importing*? I can't remember.

It was after that I met an amateur historian, of slight acquaintance, in the pub near where I live, and I asked him, in very general terms, about Becket and everything else. He told me the story of the Pilgrim's Way and suggested that I talk to you if I wanted to know more.

The reason I did, in the end, contact you for the first time was that, since Sir Richard's visit, a number of rather disturbing things began to happen. My home was broken into and – although nothing was actually taken – there was a great deal of mess, far more than was quite necessary to search everything. Nobody gets burgled where I live. It was a shock.

The following day I looked up, as I was going home, to see two men in brown macs behind me and obviously intent on what I was doing. I dodged into the post office and out through the alleyway at the back, but by the time I had reached my own road, they were there again. They stood outside my house, very obviously making notes and speaking into earpieces or something. It was extremely unnerving.

I then had a rather aggressive visit by the police, who accused me of failing to reply to a notice of impending prosecution for speeding, when no such thing had ever reached me. I may say, I am extremely careful about my speed.

It was then that I took the decision to contact you and we had that very enlightening phone conversation. I was fascinated, not to say excited, to discover that you had also been looking for me – even if you didn't actually know my name – you said you had been searching for this particular object I had inherited for your whole life. My main emotion at that stage was some relief that I was not entirely alone.

What you do not know is what happened next.

I had been driving to see the casket where I had lodged it, aware that it needed to be placed somewhere more secure and as soon as possible. I had told nobody where I was going, though I suppose we may have hinted at it in our conversation, which may have been overheard – I am just learning about these things.

I was driving up the M11 and had just passed Harlow, and I was overtaking a lorry in the middle lane, when I put my foot briefly on the brake to check my speed. To my horror, nothing happened. To make matters worse, the traffic was slowing down ahead of me and there were a number of flashing and shining red brake lights too.

I thought fast and hit the horn and, thank the

Lord – or perhaps the spirit of Becket (who knows?) – a small gap opened up to my left and I plunged through it straight onto the hard shoulder, where the car very rapidly came to a halt.

I sat there for a moment, calming down as the traffic rushed past, and put my head on the steering wheel. I called the AA and they took me on to where I was going – I had better not say where in case my friend reaps some kind of whirlwind – and I put the car into a garage and put myself up at a guesthouse. When I went to fetch it, the chief mechanic came out to see me.

"Do you have any reason to believe someone dislikes you?" he said.

"Certainly not," I said, or something of the kind.

"It's just that, if I was you, I would be careful. I don't see this very often and last time I saw it I called the police. Because I would swear that someone had cut the brake cable deliberately. It shows no sign of wear and tear and it's a clean cut."

I began to shake violently. I made up some cock and bull story about having an incompetent garage back home. The last thing I wanted to do was to draw any more attention to myself so, as you may remember, I called and asked for your address.

That is why I put the casket into the bag and, using a hire car at random, I drove to south London and deposited it where you will no doubt have found it. I hope the key arrived safely and that you will know what do about it.

I feel guilty, of course, that I may be placing you in the same kind of danger that I found myself in. I do not pretend to understand what murderous forces have been unleashed by my unwittingly bringing the casket and its contents back to England. I accept that it may have something to do with this blessed referendum – Sir Richard implied as much during our rather unpleasant interview – but it is beyond me what the link might be. I am praying that you are better equipped than myself for navigating this particular minefield and that I can say with all honesty that I no longer have the item in question. But I feel that I have done my duty to my great aunt Cecile, and you will know better than most how this relic might be protected.

I repeat my offer of money for your expenses. You have only to ask. I will be in contact later about a safe way to get in touch with me.

In the meantime, I ask your forgiveness for ducking this responsibility myself, but I am not as young as I was and I have always led a somewhat sheltered life. I am going back to France to get away from the current climate and may be there some time. I don't want to make it easy for Sir Richard if I can possibly avoid it.

But let me end with one piece of advice. The referendum is in only a few weeks' time and, before it takes place, I believe – for reasons beyond my understanding – that the relic that is now in your safekeeping has some intense dangers for its guardian. Please be careful and cover your tracks, and I would suggest also that you lie low until the vote is over and you may then be able more safely to find it a secure resting place.

I am enormously grateful for your help and advice, and for the brief moments of friendship – if I may be so bold as to describe it as that – which we enjoyed hitherto over the telephone.

Yours very sincerely,

Gerald de Stone
Fellow, Chartered Institute of Librarians and Information Professionals

XIII

"Then came its ruin. The grip of the crown caught up all the string of towns and villages and palaces and abbeys. You see the fatal date, '20th November, 29th Henry VIII.' recurring time and time again.
Otford is seized, Wrotham is seized, Boxley, Hollingbourne, Lenham, Charing, and with these six great bases, a hundred detached and smaller things: barns, fields, mills, cells – all the way along this wonderful lane the memory of the catastrophe is scarred over the history of the country-side like the old mark of a wound, till you get to poor Canterbury itself and find it empty, with nothing but antiquarian guesses to tell you of what happened to the shrine and the bones of St Thomas."
Hilaire Belloc, *The Old Road*, page 224.

"Barley! How unexpected! I didn't even dare hope I might see you as well." A bronzed man with a shaven head bounded down the gangway and onto the dockside, bobbing up and down amidst the slapping of lanyards on hundreds of aluminium masts in

Chichester Marina.

Adrian liked the man immediately, even as he realised who he was. This was Rob, Barley's estranged husband. It had to be, and it was a bit of a revelation requiring some quick re-thinking. Yes, he was an investment banker. Yes, life had been unnecessarily good to him. But he was delighted to see her, and genuinely so. That fact glowed out of him. Who really left who, Adrian wondered. I never really asked why, either. He had hated the man without even meeting him and now, ironically, he was going to need him.

"Rob, this is Adrian," shouted Barley from the dockside. "I couldn't say anything about this on the online, because it's a little – well, you know, price sensitive. So to speak."

Adrian grinned inside. That's how you get an investment banker to keep secrets, I suppose.

"How do you do, Adrian. Delighted to meet you. Anything I can do to help, I'd be only too happy. Would you like a lift or something?"

"Rob, calm down a minute will you?" Barley interrupted him. "This is a big favour I'm going to ask and it isn't against the law or anything, but can you take me with you? Adrian needs to take something to France, something valuable, back to its rightful owner, and I'm going to take it. But can you take me? I'd be ever so grateful."

"Adrian, I heard a lot about you over the years. You were big college friends, weren't you? Of course I'll help, but we need to get a move on if we're going to catch the tide. The children are aboard, not that they're children any longer. Barley, get aboard?"

Barley shuffled halfway up the gangway and took the holdall, surprised by its weight.

"Are you sure, Barley? I know how much time you've missed at work." Adrian stood pathetically, feeling guilty. "Just be very careful. I don't think they know where I am, but they can probably track me eventually."

She smiled at him indulgently.

"Adrian. I've led you a merry dance over the years. It was time I paid you back by taking part in one of your merry dances." She laughed.

"You know what to do with it, right?"

"Oh yes," she patted her pocket. "I've got the address here."

"Adrian!" shouted Rob from the stern. "Can you throw me that rope?"

The idea of going by sea had come to Adrian by a process of elimination as he had agonised about how to get the casket and Becket's head out of the country, preferably immediately.

There was the option to hide it, of course, but that would put anyone who helped him at risk as well. As the mean dwellings of south London, backing onto the railway lines, each worth at least half a million pounds, seemed to clatter past the train into London that morning, Adrian had puzzled out whether he had any means of rescuing this dangerously symbolic relic.

It really wasn't practical to post it out of the country. It was illegal to send an ancient artefact like that, and it would be X-rayed and seized by customs' officials. It wasn't practical either to take it on a plane. The same would apply and he was too vulnerable to intervention at the last minute by the ODF. He could drive onto a ferry but possibly the same would happen there. What he really needed was somebody with their own boat. By the time he had reached Victoria, he had reached his decision. Wasn't Barley taking the children down to her ex-husband's yacht later that day?

He appeared not to have been followed, but he could not take the risk that he wasn't. So he called Barley on the pre-arranged code. Two rings, then he put the receiver down and waited to reach her next-door neighbour. He knew there was still a phone box in Victoria Street. He wrenched open the door – how long was it since he had been in one of these? He could barely remember how they worked. He had three pound coins. Even so, he knew they could be listening in, so it had to be a clipped conversation.

"Barley, how are you?"

"Adrian! I'm fine, fine. But how are you, did you...?

"Did I – yes I did and I've got a great deal to tell you, and some answers. But listen, Barley, what time do your kids go? I mean what time do they set off... with your ex, what's his name... Rob?"

"Later this afternoon. I have to take them. Why?"

"Then we just have time. Do you think...? I mean, could you bear to go with them, if you take something with you? I badly need you to deliver something, you see."

"Well, of course. If you think so."

"I mean, it won't be too painful for you? And he won't be too, I don't know... angry?"

"No, we're very friendly really. Of course, I want to help."

Adrian breathed a sigh of relief. He could see what he had to do.

"That's wonderful. Thank you so much. I'll meet you down there – don't say where – I know where he is..."

He ended the call, with a huge sense of escape. If

this could just work out, he could see a way through. He could have done none of this if it hadn't been for Barley, but there was no doubt from Mr de Stone's letter that they were both in danger now. It had made it very clear that the ODF were prepared to do almost anything, and it confirmed his suspicion that Peter Shilling's death had been no accident.

There was just one slim hope that he might wrong-foot them by making them over-react.

He walked further down Victoria Street to buy a replica of the holdall Mr de Stone had used, which he was now carrying in his hand. At great expense, he also bought a large metal ornament, roughly the same shape and size as the casket. He put one inside the other and set off at a fierce pace to Horse Guards.

He was nodded through by security, but he stood a few minutes at the door to the Treasury, hoping perhaps, that he might finally be seen. He darted inside, up in the lift until he reached the office of the Permanent Secretary. Then he ran off ten copies of the letter from Mr de Stone.

"Donna, could I just leave these here? It contains something I want to discuss with the CST when I'm back. He hasn't asked for it, but I am hoping to arrange a meeting with him. Is that OK?"

"Do you want me to check the Chief Secretary's diary?" asked Donna.

"Can we do that when I get back?"

Adrian felt a little guilty as he stashed the letters in the corner by the Permanent Secretary's PA. What would happen? Actually, he had no idea."

Next, he popped in to see Nadia to tell her an edited version of what happened.

"You are insane, Adrian."

"I know, but look – could you look after one of these letters – just in case something happens to me? And can I leave this holdall in our office?"

"As I said. You are crazy."

"Listen, Nadia. This is very important. After I've gone, can you go to one of the open plan desks and lock the door to your office? Don't ask me why; it's a precaution – but please do it."

"OK, OK. But tell me all about it afterwards, won't you. You know those OFT people came to see me and asked me to tell them next time you came in?"

"They did? Perfect!" Why not take the opportunity? *Nadia* could tell them he was in. It would sound much more authentic.

"Can you give me half an hour and then tell them I was here. Tell them I had a big blue holdall with me? Then go out. Lock the door, remember...?"

"OK, if you're sure. You are sure, right?"

"But look, Nadia. If anything happens, here I mean, then can you take this letter to the Permanent Secretary, in confidence, by way of explanation?

"Yes, yes, just put it there can you? Now, if you don't mind, some of us have got real work to do..."

"One other thing. If anyone asks for me, could you just tell them I'm at my desk? And make sure you're out when they come. Please. Just in case."

Finally, he went to his old desk, next door to where Nadia sat and away from the open plan office. He closed the door and grinned at her across the space. He stashed the new holdall underneath and lifted the receiver. He would have to take the risk that Barley had already left.

Her answerphone clicked in.

"Barley, just a message to say I've got to work and I'm here now and, yes, I've got it under my desk. Nadia's looking after it. See you whenever."

Was that authentic enough? It had to be. Then he picked up the holdall with the real casket and, waving behind him, he left. He had about an hour, he calculated, before they arrived. Next was the really difficult part – getting out of the Treasury by way of the network of tunnels that ran from the basement down Whitehall, and without causing a security incident at 10 Downing Street if he came up unexpectedly under there.

"Rather a peculiar call I had about you Adrian," said his boss, as they passed in the corridor a moment or so later. "You're not in any kind of trouble are you? I confess I couldn't quite see what they were driving at."

"No, I'm fine, thank you. Rather a tiresome run-in I had with a quango connected to the Palace and linked to the work we were doing on inquests. I don't think we need worry any more."

"Good to hear it. Good holiday by the way? I don't feel I've seen you for weeks."

"Really brilliant, thank you – I walked the Pilgrim's Way!"

He knew vaguely where the tunnels were. He had opened a door in the basement and followed the passage, past the IT department, stashed away where nobody could find them, and through another door marked 'No Admittance'. As far as he could tell, it was heading in the right direction, which meant up Whitehall, dead straight, under wires and pipework that looked as if it had survived from the days of the Blitz when so much government work took place underground. Pieces of Crown Estate's asbestos, seeking whom it could infect, fell around him.

There was a dead end, an unexpected right turn

and another door and he found himself in an identical basement. Perhaps this was the moment to risk coming to the surface, up the bare linoleum-covered stairs and into another bland government department, with people ambling along towards the coffee machines. But which one?

A glance at the notices confirmed his suspicions. He had navigated correctly but perhaps not far enough. This was the Foreign Office. All he needed to do now was to wangle his way out of security and onto the street. He glanced at his watch. There was still time to get to Victoria Station and to Barley and the children, and the marina.

As he handed over the heavy holdall to Barley on the bobbing marina boards beside Rob's yacht, he squeezed her hand. "You're a lifesaver. Maybe literally, but be careful. They don't know where I am – yet. I've made them think I'm still at the Treasury, with this." He nodded at Becket's last remains on earth. "I asked Nadia to give them a message from me."

"Just be careful, OK? Now that I've met you again, I don't want to lose you."

"I will, and you be careful too. You know where you're going? Straight to the Louvre. I've put the numbers of my friend there on the letter – and when you read the letter, you'll know all you need to know."

Rob's energetic and bouncy face, popping up and down along the deck, was a bit of a distraction, and a constraint too.

"This has been an amazing adventure, and now I think and hope it's going to be over. The referendum's in a couple of days too – I hope you voted before you went?"

"Oh no, I forgot. Will you vote for me?"

"I can't, can I?" Was she asking him to commit electoral fraud?

"I mean vote with extra passion for me as well."

"Oh, I see," said Adrian, aware suddenly that this was a kind of flirtation and struggling to respond. "Of course. Barley – um, when you're back...?"

But the engine roared and Rob was upon them and, through the cacophony, Barley was waving and clutching the holdall, which had caused so much trouble for so many centuries, to her breast.

"I say, could you just let go that rope?"

"OK, Rob," said Adrian, waving sadly back, as he threw the rope on the deck and the yacht began to make its way into open water.

XIV

"When noon was long past, we set out from Winchester, without any pack or burden to explore the hundred and twenty miles before us, not knowing what we might find, and very eager."
Hilaire Belloc, *The Old Road*, page 114.

A strange calmness had come upon Adrian as he sat back in his seat on the train from Chichester, which took its unhurried and apologetic way to Victoria Station.

He had no illusions. If, as he suspected, Sheldrake and his men would overplay their hand in the Treasury, searching for his room, they could possibly be stupid enough – if not desperate enough – to respond to Nadia's information about where he was and that he had secreted a holdall in the Treasury, with their automatic weapons. If, as he hoped, Sheldrake went too far, he knew what would happen.

There would be an internal security inquiry which would involve a slapping of the wrists and maybe a review of the ODF. Perhaps it would be the end of his career, but it should also be the end of Sir Richard and his gang. The world would know nothing. The establishment doesn't wash its dirty linen in public, after all. He knew that very well. When the fuss had died down and the referendum was won or lost, then he was – in the end – in a more powerful position than Sir Richard.

He might not ever have evidence to have the man arrested for the murder of his friend, as he should be, but he would make sure – if he kept his job – that the review into the finances of missing quangos like the Office of the Defender of the Faith was a pretty brutal affair. He could make sure that sunlight finally burst into these fetid, forgotten corners of bigotry. He could and he would. If, as seemed likely, Sheldrake was even then storming into the Treasury, then he would be on the losing side.

The motion of the train was beginning to lull him to sleep. What was more interesting to him at that moment was what Barley would do. She would take the casket to Le Monde and then on to the Louvre, and they would immediately see its significance, and they would preserve it. But after that – might they have some kind of future together?

There had been the occasional passionate embrace, even kissing, after Peter's dinners in days gone by. Could they recapture that possibility? He had thought himself past longings of this kind, but found that he was now aching for her to come home. These things only matter if you fail to act on them. He had no idea of her feelings on the subject, she was at least undecided and probably lukewarm, but this time – this time – he was going to try.

The train drew into Horsham. He could just see a copy of the *Evening Standard* in someone's arm. He strained to see the front page. Then he caught sight of a front page on the seat next to him. Why had he not noticed it before? The headline said: 'SHOOTING AT THE TREASURY'.

They had passed Gatwick Airport now and the North Downs loomed ahead of them, and as the train sped on towards London, he looked up and then he saw it. He knew it could not be real, and yet could it have come from his imagination either? There it was, unmistakably so, a line of light across the hill and halfway up, so that the water would drain off, and leading, he knew, to Canterbury. There it was. The Old Road, shining its way to him across the centuries.

By the same author...

David Boyle

Regicide

Peter Abelard and the Great Jewel

England, 1100. King William Rufus is killed with an arrow on a hunt. Rumours start immediately that he was murdered. Nineteen years later, in France, the poet Hilary the Englishman meets a strange man who offers to buy Hilary a meal if he does him a favour. He gives Hilary a pouch of silver, and a message to be delivered to Count Fulk in Anjou. But by morning the man is dead, and the crows are feasting on his body.

Fearing he will be accused of murder, Hilary flees. But now he is pursued himself, and also by the murderers. He knows only one man can help him. His former teacher, the brilliant Peter Abelard...

This is a rollicking chase, a hunt for the truth before it is too late - for Hilary to save his own life and the lives of many. It is also a medieval detective adventure in the style of Umberto Eco, Ellis Peters and Ken Follett. It brings the early twelfth century to glorious life.

"There are so many great characters (real and fictional) and the narrative prose is so strong that it's easy to get carried away with this book, completely forgetting that there is a real world out there!"
Amazon review

Other titles by David Boyle

Building Futures

Funny Money: In search of alternative cash

The Sum of our Discontent

The Tyranny of Numbers

The Money Changers

Authenticity: Brands, Fakes, Spin and the Lust for
Real Life

Blondel's Song

Leaves the World to Darkness (fiction)

Toward the Setting Sun

The New Economics: A Bigger Picture (with
Andrew Simms)

Money Matters: Putting the eco into economics

The Wizard

Eminent Corporations (with Andrew Simms)

Voyages of Discovery

The Human Element

On the Eighth Day, God Created Allotments

The Age to Come

Unheard, Unseen: Submarine E14 and the
Dardanelles

Broke: Who killed the middle classes?

Alan Turing: Unlocking the Enigma

Rupert Brooke: The Last Patriot
Jerusalem: England's National Anthem
Give and Take (with Sarah Bird)
People Powered Prosperity (with Tony Greenham)
Rupert Brooke: England's Last Patriot
How to be English
Operation Primrose
Before Enigma
The Piper (fiction)
Scandal
How to become a freelance writer
V for Victory
Lost at Sea
Regicide (fiction)
The Death of Liberal Democracy?
(with Joe Zammit-Lucia)
Prosperity Parade
Cancelled!
Like leaves fall in Autumn: Hotspur, Henry IV and
the Battle of Shrewsbury
Ronald Laing: The rise and fall and rise of a
revolutionary psychiatrist

See also our website at
www.therealpress.co.uk